Her best friend is gone . . .
but she left something behind.

I get down on the carpet to look under my bed. I stick my arm under and feel around, find a couple mismatched socks, and something I don't recognize—hard and flat and dusty. I pull it out, thinking maybe it's a yearbook from elementary school, and then I see it and my heart stops.

Ingrid's journal.

For some reason, I feel afraid. It's like I'm split down the middle and one half of me wants to open it more than I've ever wanted to do anything. The other half is so scared. I can't stop shaking.

Did it get kicked under the bed one night by accident?

Did she hide it?

I stare at it in my hands forever, just feeling its weight, looking at the place where one Wite-Out wing is starting to flake off. Then, once my hands are steadied, I open to the first page. It's a drawing of her face—yellow hair; blue eyes; small, crooked smile. She's looking straight ahead. Birds fly across the background. She drew them blurry, to show movement, and across the top she wrote, *Me on a Sunday Morning.*

I turn the page.

As I read, I can hear Ingrid's voice, hushed and fast, like she's telling me secrets.

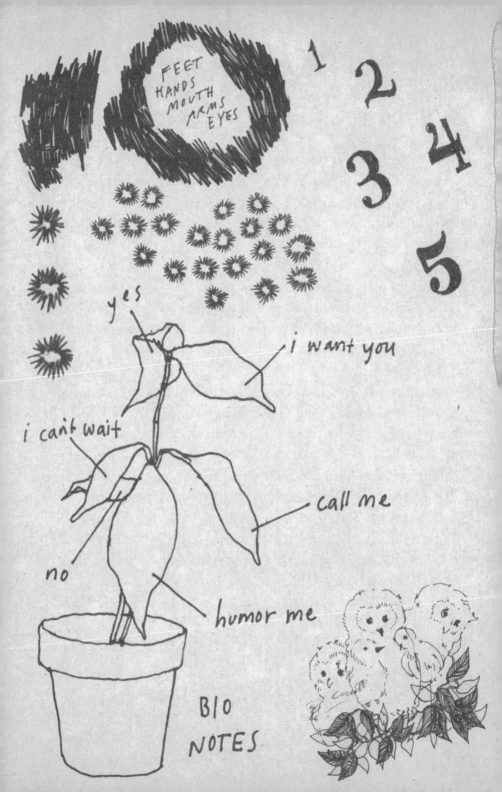

OTHER BOOKS YOU MAY ENJOY

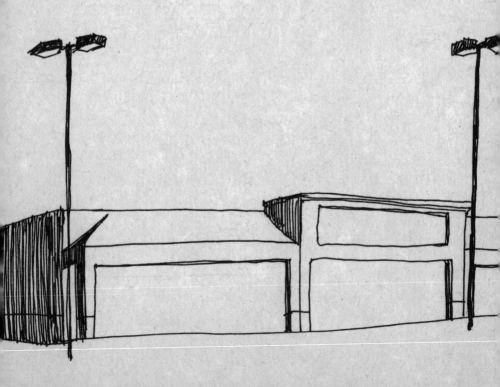

hold still

Nina LaCour

with ILLUSTRATIONS by MIA NOLTING

speak

An Imprint of Penguin Group (USA) Inc.

SPEAK
Published by the Penguin Group
Penguin Group (USA) Inc., 345 Hudson Street, New York, New York 10014, U.S.A.
Penguin Group (Canada), 90 Eglinton Avenue East, Suite 700, Toronto, Ontario, Canada M4P 2Y3
(a division of Pearson Penguin Canada Inc.)
Penguin Books Ltd, 80 Strand, London WC2R 0RL, England
Penguin Ireland, 25 St Stephen's Green, Dublin 2, Ireland (a division of Penguin Books Ltd)
Penguin Group (Australia), 250 Camberwell Road, Camberwell, Victoria 3124, Australia
(a division of Pearson Australia Group Pty Ltd)
Penguin Books India Pvt Ltd, 11 Community Centre, Panchsheel Park, New Delhi - 110 017, India
Penguin Group (NZ), 67 Apollo Drive, Rosedale, North Shore 0632, New Zealand
(a division of Pearson New Zealand Ltd.)
Penguin Books (South Africa) (Pty) Ltd, 24 Sturdee Avenue, Rosebank, Johannesburg 2196, South Africa

Registered Offices: Penguin Books Ltd, 80 Strand, London WC2R 0RL, England

First published in the United States of America by Dutton Books,
a member of Penguin Group (USA) Inc., 2009

Published by Speak, an imprint of Penguin Group (USA) Inc., 2010

3 5 7 9 10 8 6 4

Text copyright © Nina LaCour, 2009
Illustrations copyright © Mia Nolting, 2009
All rights reserved

THE LIBRARY OF CONGRESS HAS CATALOGED THE DUTTON BOOKS EDITION AS FOLLOWS:
LaCour, Nina.
Hold still / Nina LaCour ; with illustrations by Mia Nolting.
229 p. : ill. ; 24 cm.
Summary: Ingrid didn't leave a note. Three months after her best friend's suicide,
Caitlin finds what she left instead: a journal, hidden under Caitlin's bed.
ISBN: 978-0-525-42155-9 (hc)
[1. Bereavement—Juvenile fiction. 2. Suicide—Juvenile fiction. 3. Friendship—Juvenile fiction.
4. Psychological fiction. 5. Bereavement—Fiction. 6. Suicide—Fiction. 7. Friendship—Fiction.]
[Fic]—dc22   2010275162

Speak ISBN 978-0-14-241694-5

Designed by Heather Wood
Text set in Minion

Printed in the United States of America

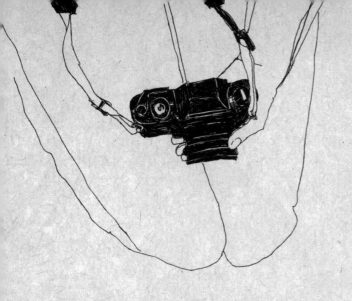

for my family and for Kristyn

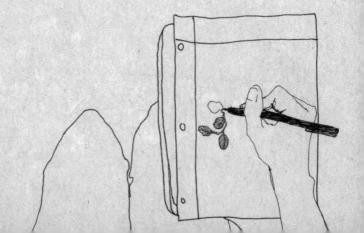

hold still

summer

1

I watch drops of water fall from the ends of my hair. They streak down my towel, puddle on the sofa cushion. My heart pounds so hard I can feel it in my ears.

"Sweetheart. Listen."

Mom says Ingrid's name and I start to hum, not the melody to a song, just one drawn-out note. I know it makes me seem crazy, I know it won't make anything change, but it's better than crying, it's better than screaming, it's better than listening to what they're telling me.

Something is smashing my chest—an anchor, gravity. Soon I'll cave in on myself. I stumble upstairs and yank on the jeans and tank top I wore yesterday. Then I'm out the door, up the street, around the corner to the bus stop. Dad calls my name but I don't shout back. Instead, I step onto the bus just as its doors are shutting. I find a seat in the back and ride away, through Los Cerros and through the next town, until I'm on an unfamiliar street, and that's where I get off. I sit on the bench at the bus stop, try to slow my breathing. The light here is different, bluer. A smiling mom with a baby in a stroller glides past me. A tree branch moves in the breeze. I try to be as light as air.

But my hands are wild, they need to move, so I pick at a piece of the bench where the wood is splintering. I break a short nail on my right hand even shorter, but I manage to pull off a small piece of wood. I drop it into my cupped palm and pry off another.

All last night, I listened to a recording of my voice reciting biology facts on repeat. It plays back in my head now, a sound track for catastrophe, and drowns everything out. *If a brown-eyed man and a brown-eyed woman have a child, the child will probably have brown eyes. But if both the father and the mother have a gene for blue eyes, it's possible that their child could have blue eyes.*

An old guy in a snowflake cardigan sits next to me. My hand is now half full of wooden strips. I feel him watching but I can't stop. I want to say, *What are you staring at? It's hot, it's June, and you're wearing a Christmas sweater.*

"Do you need help, darling?" the old guy asks. His mustache is wispy and white.

Without looking from the bench, I shake my head. *No.*

He takes a cell phone from his pocket. "Would you like to use my phone?"

My heart beats off rhythm and it makes me cough.

"May I call your mother?"

Ingrid has blond hair. She has blue eyes, which means that even though her father's eyes are brown, he must have a recessive blue-eye gene.

A bus nears. The old guy stands, wavers.

"Darling," he says.

He lifts his hand as if he's going to pat my shoulder, but changes his mind.

My left hand is all the way full of wood now, and it's starting to spill over. I am not a darling. I am a girl ready to explode into nothing.

The old guy backs away, boards the bus, vanishes from sight.

The cars pass in front of me. One blur of color after another. Sometimes they stop at the light or for someone to cross the street, but they always go away eventually. I think I'll live here, stay like this forever, pick away at the bench until it's a pile of splinters on the sidewalk. Forget what it feels like to care about anyone.

A bus rolls up but I wave it past. A few minutes later, two little girls peer at me from the backseat of a blue car—one is blond and fair; one is brunette, darker. Colored barrettes decorate their hair. It isn't impossible that they're sisters, but it's unlikely. Their heads tilt to see me better. They stare hard. When the light changes to green, they reach their small hands out the rolled-down window and wave so hard and fast that it looks like birds have bloomed from their wrists.

Sometime later, my dad pulls up. He leans to the passenger side and pushes the door open. The smell of leather. Thin, cold, air-conditioned air. I climb in. Let him take me home.

2

I sleep through the next day. Each time I go to the bathroom, I try not to look in the mirror. Once, I catch my reflection: it looks like I've been punched in both eyes.

3

I can't talk about the day that follows that.

4

We wind up Highway 1 at a crawl because Dad is a cautious driver and he's terrified of heights. Below us to one side are rocks and ocean; to the other, dense trees and signs welcoming us to towns with populations of eighty-four. Mom has brought her entire classical CD collection, and now we're on Beethoven. It's "Für Elise," which she always plays on her piano. Fingers dance softly across her lap.

On the outskirts of a small town, we pull off the road to eat lunch. We sit on an old quilt. Mom and Dad look at me and I look at the worn fabric, the hand-sewn stitches.

"There are things you should know," Mom says.

I listen for the cars passing by, and the waves, and the crinkling of paper sandwich wrappers. Still, some of their words make it through: *clinically depressed; medication; since she was nine years old.* The ocean is far below us, but the waves crash so loudly, sound close enough to drown us.

"Caitlin?" Dad says.

Mom touches my knee. "Sweetheart?" she asks. "Are you listening?"

At night, we stay in a cabin with bunk beds and walls made of tree trunks split open. I brush my teeth with my back to the mirror, climb up the ladder to the top bunk, and pretend to fall asleep. My parents creak through the cabin, turning on and off the faucet, flushing the toilet, unzipping their duffel bags. I pull my legs to my chest, try to inhabit as little space as possible.

The room goes dark.

I open my eyes to the tree-trunk wall. Once I learned that trees grow from the inside out. A circle of wood for each year. I count them with my fingers.

"This will be good for her," Dad says softly.

"I hope so."

"At least it will get her away from home. It's quiet here."

Mom whispers, "She's hardly spoken for days."

I hold still and stop counting. I wait to hear more, but minutes pass, and then the whistle of Dad's snore begins, followed by Mom's even breaths.

My hands lose track of the years. It's too dark to start over.

At three or four in the morning, I jolt awake. I fix my eyes to constellations that have been painted on the ceiling. I try not to blink for too long because when I do I see Ingrid's face, eyes shut and lips still. I mouth biology facts to keep my head clear. *There are two stages of meiosis and then four daughter cells are produced,* I whisper almost silently, careful not to wake my parents up. *Each of the daughter cells has half the chromosomes of the parent cells.* Outside, a car passes. Light sweeps over the ceiling, across the stars. I repeat the facts until all the words cram together.

Twostagesofmeiosisandthenfourdaughtercellsareproducedeachdaughtercellhashalfthechromosomesoftheparentcellstwostagesofmeiosis . . .

Pretty soon I start to smile. It sounds funnier and funnier each time I say it. And then I have to grab my pillow and bury my face so my parents don't wake to the sound of me laughing myself to sleep.

5

On a hot morning in July, Dad rents a car because he has to go back to work. But Mom and I stay in Northern California like it's the only place we've heard of. I sit in front and navigate, keeping us within the invisible boundaries on the map—no farther north than a few miles into Oregon, no farther south than Chico. We spend the summer wandering through caves and forests, surviving crooked roads, and eating grilled-cheese sandwiches at roadside restaurants. We only talk about the things right in front of us—the redwoods, the waitresses, the strength of our iced teas. One night, we discover a tiny old movie theater in the middle of nowhere. We see a children's movie because it's the only thing playing, and pay more attention to the kids laughing and yelling than we do to the screen. Twice, we strap flashlights to our heads and grope through lava caves in Lassen National Park. Mom trips and shrieks. Her voice echoes forever. I start dreaming about the cardigan man. In the middle of the forest, he drifts toward me in a tux with a red bow tie. *Darling,* he says, and holds out his phone. I know Ingrid's on the other end, waiting for me to talk to her. As I reach for it, I notice—surrounding me are green trees, brown earth, but I am in black-and-white.

In the mornings, Mom lets me drink coffee and says, "Honey, you're pale."

6

And then, out of nowhere, September comes.

We have to go back.

fall

1

It is 3 A.M. Not the most logical time to take a photograph without
lights or a flash or high-speed film, but here I am anyway, perched
on the hood of the boxy gray car I should be able to drive by now,
camera tilted to the sky, hoping to catch the moon before a cloud
moves across it. I snap frame after frame at slow shutter speeds until the moon is gone and the sky is black.

My car creaks as I slide off, moans when I open the door and
climb into the back. I push down the lock and curl up across the
cloth seats.

I have five hours to get okay.

Fifteen minutes go by. I'm pulling the fake fur from the front
seat covers even though I love them. I can't stop my fingers; white
tufts are falling everywhere.

By four-thirty I've thrown several thrashing fits, given myself a
headache, put my fist in my mouth and screamed. I need to get the
pressure out of my body somehow so I can finally fall asleep.

In the house, my bedroom light clicks on. Then the light in the kitchen. The door swings open and my mom appears, clutching the collar of her robe. I reach between the seats and over to my flashers, click them twice, watch her shuffle back inside. I have one frame left, so through the windshield I take a picture of the dark house with its two lit-up rooms. I'll title it: *My House at 5:23* A.M. Maybe I'll look at it one day when my head isn't pounding and try to make sense of why, for every night since I got home, I've locked myself in a cold car just a few steps outside my warm house, where my parents are so worried they can't sleep, either.

Sometime around six I start dreaming.

My dad wakes me with his knuckles tapping my window. I open my eyes to the morning light. He's in his suit already. "Looks like there's been a blizzard in here," he says.

The backs of the seat covers are furless. My hand aches.

2

I walk the long way to school, my new schedule folded into the smallest square and stuffed deep in my pocket. I pass the strip mall; the Safeway and its sprawling parking lot; the lot of land for sale where the bowling alley was before the town decided bowling wasn't important, and leveled it. On a Friday night two years ago, I darted onto one of the lanes and took a picture of Ingrid sending a heavy red ball toward me. It rushed between my feet as I stood there, one foot in each gutter. The owner yelled at us and kicked us out but later on forgave us. I have the photograph on my closet door: a blur of red, Ingrid's eyes fierce and determined. Behind her: lights, strangers, rows of bowling shoes.

I stop at a corner to read the headlines through the glass of a newspaper box. Something must be going on in the world: floods, medical breakthroughs, war? But this morning, like most mornings, all the *Los Cerros Tribune* has to offer me is local politics and hot weather.

As soon as I can, I get away from the street because I don't want anyone to see me and pull over to offer a ride. They would probably want to talk about Ingrid and I would just stare at my hands like an idiot. Or they wouldn't want to talk about Ingrid and instead there would be a long silence that would get heavier and heavier.

On the trail between the condos comes the sound of wheels on gravel, and then Taylor Riley is next to me on his skateboard, looking so much taller than before. He doesn't say anything. I watch my shoes kick up dirt. He rolls past me, then waits for me to catch up. He does this over and over, saying nothing, not even looking at me.

His hair is sun-bleached and his skin is tanned and freckled. He could play a version himself on a sitcom—the most popular boy in school, oblivious to his own perfection. His TV self would trade his skateboard for a football jacket. Instead of sitting around looking bored, he would win trophies. He'd be driving to school in some expensive car with a smiling homecoming queen in the passenger seat, not following a narrow dirt path alongside a quiet, sullen girl.

The path ends and spills us out onto the sidewalk. A block away, everyone is pulling into the high school parking lot. I want to turn and run back home.

"Hey, sorry about Ingrid," Taylor says.

Automatically, I say, "Thanks."

Car after car passes us and turns into the parking lot. All the girls are squealing and hugging as if it's been years since they've laid eyes on one another. The guys are slamming their hands down on one another's backs, which I guess is supposed to mean something nice. I try not to look at them. Taylor and I face each other, each of us looking at his skateboard standing still on the ground. A car door slams. Footsteps. Alicia McIntosh collides into me with her arms open.

"Caitlin," she whispers.

Her perfume is strong and flowery. I try not to choke.

She takes a step back, holds me by the elbows. She's wearing tight jeans and a yellow tank top with QUEEN written in blue sequins across her chest. Her red hair skims the tops of her shoulders.

"You are so strong," she says, "to come back to school. If I were you I would be . . . I don't know. I'd still be hiding in bed, I guess, with the blankets pulled up over my head."

She stares at me with a look that's supposed to be meaningful. Her big green eyes stretch even bigger. In my one semester of drama, the teacher taught us that if a person keeps her eyes open long enough, she'll start to cry. I wonder if Alicia has forgotten that we were in the same class. She keeps squeezing my elbows and finally a small tear trickles over her freckles.

Alicia, I want to say. *Someday you will win an Oscar.*

Instead I say, "Thanks."

She nods, wrinkling her forehead and squeezing out one last tear.

Her focus snaps away from me to something in the distance. Her crew is walking toward us. They're all wearing different versions of the same tank top. They say, PRINCESS, ANGEL, and SPOILED. I guess Alicia is the leader this year. I should feel lucky that her hands are cutting off my circulation.

"I'm going to make you late to class. But please remember. If you ever need anything, you can call me. I know we haven't hung out in a while, but we used to be really good friends. I'm here for you. Day or night."

I can't imagine ever being Alicia's friend. Not because we're so different now, but because it's impossible to think of a time before high school. Before photography and finals and the pressure of college. Before Ingrid. I remember Alicia as a little kid, hands on her hips in the sandbox, informing all the other kids that she was the only unicorn. And I remember a girl with brown braided hair and pastel corduroys galloping on the blacktop imagining she was a horse, and I know that girl was me, but it feels distant, like someone else's memory.

Now she gives my elbows one last squeeze and sets me free.

"Taylor," she says. "Are you coming?"

"Yeah, just a minute."

"We're going to be late."

"Go ahead."

She rolls her eyes. Her friends arrive and she leads them toward the English hall.

Taylor clears his throat. He glances at me, then back to his skateboard. "So I hope you don't think this is a rude question or anything, but how did she do it?"

My knees buckle. I think, *If a brown-eyed man and a brown-eyed woman have a child, the child will probably have brown eyes.* The main entrance is ahead of us, the soccer field to the left. I stick my hand in my pocket and touch my schedule. Like the last two years, I have photography first period. I will my legs to work again and, miraculously, they do. I step onto the grass, away from Taylor, and mumble, "I have to go." I picture Ms. Delani waiting for me, rising from her chair when I walk into the classroom, pushing past the other students until she gets to me. When I imagine her touching my arm, I am flooded with relief.

3

I haven't talked to Ms. Delani since everything happened. Maybe she'll excuse herself from the rest of the class and lead me to her back office, where we'll sit together and talk about how fucked life is. She won't ask if I'm okay because she'll already know that for us *Are you okay?* is an impossible question. She'll spend the period talking to the class about how sad this year is going to be. In honor of Ingrid, the first project will be about loss and everyone will know, even before I turn in my photograph, that mine will be the most heartbreaking.

I filter through the door with the rest of the kids. The classroom is brighter than I remember, and colder. Ms. Delani stands at her desk, looking as perfect and beautiful as she must every day, in crisply ironed slacks and a black sleeveless sweater. Ingrid and I used to try to picture her doing real-people stuff, like taking the garbage out and shaving her armpits. We called her by her first name whenever we were alone. *Imagine Veena,* Ingrid would say, *in sweatpants and a ratty T-shirt, getting up at one o'clock in the afternoon with a hangover.* I would try to picture it, but it was useless; instead I saw her in silk pajamas, drinking espresso in a sunny kitchen.

A few kids are already scattered around the classroom. Ms. Delani glances toward the door as I walk in, then away, quickly, like a flash went off so brightly it hurt. I wait in the doorway for a second to give her a chance to look again, but she doesn't move. Maybe she's waiting for me to go up to her? People start gathering behind me, so I take a few steps toward her and pause by the shelves of art books in the front, trying to figure out what to do.

There's no way she hasn't seen me.

Everyone's streaming in around me, and Ms. Delani is saying hi and smiling and ignoring me standing just a few feet from her. I have no idea what's happening, but being surrounded by everyone feels a little like drowning, so I walk right in front of her and hover there.

"Hi," I say.

She glances at me through the red-rimmed glasses that frame her dark eyes.

"Welcome back."

But she sounds so absent, like I'm someone she vaguely knows.

I stumble to the table where I sat last year, open my notebook, and act like I'm reading something really interesting. Maybe she's

waiting until everyone sits down and class officially starts before
she says anything about Ingrid. The last people come in and I pretend not to notice that the seat next to me, Ingrid's old seat, stays
empty.

The bell rings.

Ms. Delani scans the class. I wait for her to look over here, to
smile or nod or *anything*, but it seems like the room ends just to
the right of me. She smiles at everybody else, but I, apparently,
do not exist. It's obvious she doesn't want me here, and I have no
idea what to do. I would get my stuff together and leave, but I'd
have nowhere to go. I want to crawl under the table and hide there
until everyone is gone.

The walls are covered with our final projects from last year.
Ingrid is the only one who got three of her pictures up. They're all
next to one another, in the front of the classroom, right in the center. One is a landscape—two slopes, covered in rocks and thorny
bushes, with a creek running crookedly through them. One is a
still life of a cracked vase. And one is of me. The lighting is really
intense and I'm making a strange expression, like a grimace. I'm
not looking at the camera. In the darkroom, when Ingrid made a
print of it for the first time, we stood back and watched the image
of me appear on the wet paper, and Ingrid said, *This is so you, it's
so you*. And I said, *Oh God, it is*, even though I hardly recognized
myself. I watched shadows form beneath my eyes, an unfamiliar
curve darken at the corner of my mouth. It was a harder version of
me, a grittier version. Soon I was staring at a face that looked completely unfamiliar, nothing like a girl who grew up in a rich suburb
with loving parents and her own bathroom.

Maybe it was a premonition or something, because as I look at it
now, it makes more sense.

At first I can't find any of my pictures, but then I spot one. Ms.
Delani must really hate it to have pinned it up where it is, in the
only dark corner of the entire room, above a heater that juts out

of the wall and blocks part of it from view. Ingrid was amazing at art—she could draw and paint anything and make it look even better than it was—but I thought we were both good at photography.

When I took the picture I was sure it would be amazing. Ingrid and I were taking the BART train to see her older brother, who lives in San Francisco. It was a long ride because we live so far out in the suburbs. When we were passing through Oakland, there was some sort of delay, and for a while the train we were on sat still on the tracks. The engine stopped humming. People shifted in their seats, settled into waiting. I looked out the window, across the freeway, to where the sky looked so vibrantly blue over sad little run-down houses and industrial buildings. I took the picture. But I guess the colors were the beautiful part. In black-and-white it's just sad, and Ms. Delani is probably right—who wants to look at that? But it's still so embarrassing to have it stuck in a corner. There are a million pictures up there, but right now I feel like there's a neon sign around mine. I try to think of some way to sneak it off the wall.

All through class, Ms. Delani smiles while she's talking about the high expectations she has of her advanced students, smiles so hard her cheeks must hurt. The ancient clock on the wall behind me ticks so slowly. I stare at it for a few seconds, wishing the period over, and notice all the cubbies in the back of the room. I never got to empty mine last year because I missed the final week of school.

Ms. Delani writes review terms on the board—*aperture, light meter, shutter speed*. I start getting all fidgety, thinking of all the things I have in my cubby. I know I have some old photos, and I think there might be a few of Ingrid. I glance at the clock again, and the minute hand has hardly moved. I should wait until class is over, but I just don't really care about being polite right now. Ms. Delani isn't exactly being polite. So I scoot my chair back, ignore the sound of metal scraping against linoleum, and stand up. A couple people turn to see what's going on, but when they realize it's me they turn back fast, as if accidental eye contact could be deadly. Ms. Delani just keeps talking like everything's normal, like she isn't completely ignoring the fact that Ingrid's not here. She doesn't even pause when I walk over to my cubby and start pulling pictures out. Because I'm feeling so daring, I don't go straight back to my seat. Instead, I take my time sorting through a bunch of old pictures I'd forgotten about. Some of Ingrid's are mixed in, the ones I wanted copies of, and I look through them until I find my favorite—a hill with grass on it and little wildflowers, blue sky. It must be the most peaceful picture in the world. It's the setting of a fairy tale, it's somewhere that can't exist anymore.

I turn around, all these photographs of my old life in my hands, and I get a sudden urge to scream. I can see myself doing it, screaming so loudly that Ms. Delani's perfect glasses shatter, all the photographs fly off the wall, everyone in the class goes deaf. She would have to look at me then. But instead I walk back to my seat and lay my head down on the cold desk.

When the bell rings, everyone gets up and leaves. Ms. Delani says good-bye to some people, but not to invisible me.

4

This is what I can't stop thinking about this morning:

Freshman year. First period. I sat next to a girl I hadn't seen before. She was scribbling in a journal, drawing all these curvy designs. When I sat down next to her she glanced up at me and smiled. I liked the earrings she was wearing. They were red and looked like buttons.

We had spent the morning crammed in the gym with the whole school listening to the principal, Mr. Nelson, give us a pep talk. Mr. Nelson had this round face, small mouth, enormous eyes. He was balding and what was left of his hair was kind of tufty. If it's possible for a person to look like an owl, then that's what he looked like. I had felt lost, the gym seemed colossal, even the kids from my old middle school looked like strangers. Now we were in photography class, and even though I had never taken a film photograph or really even learned anything about art, I felt so much more comfortable in Ms. Delani's classroom than I had felt a few minutes before. Ms. Delani called the first name off her roster and continued down the list, making notes and taking forever. I saw the girl rip a page out of her journal and write something. She pushed it closer to me. It said, *Four years of this shit? Dear lord save us.*

I grabbed her pen and tried to think of something cool to say. I was the new me. Braver. I had on these glass bracelets that chimed when I moved my arm.

I wrote, *If you had to make out with any guy in the school who would it be?*

Immediately, she wrote, *Principal Nelson, of course. He's such a hottie!*

When I read it I had to laugh. I tried to make it sound like I was coughing and Ms. Delani looked up from her roster to tell us that in her mind we were all adults now, and didn't have to ask for permission to go out into the hall if we needed a drink of water or to use the restroom.

So I did. I walked out, feeling how straight my hair was, how great my pants fit, how nice my bracelets sounded. I bent down and I drank the cold drinking-fountain water and I felt like, *This is it. My life is starting.* And when I got back to my seat there was a new note that said, *I'm Ingrid.*

I'm Caitlin, I wrote back.

And then we were friends. It was that easy.

5

I have English with Mr. Robertson last period. When I walk in he doesn't give me any fake looks. He just nods at me, smiles and says, "Welcome back, Caitlin."

Henry Lucas, who is possibly the most popular guy in the junior class, and also probably the meanest, sits in the far back corner, ignoring a couple of Alicia's followers. ANGEL flicks her pink, manicured nails through his black hair and SPOILED says, "So you're gonna have a thing on Friday, right?"

Henry's always having parties because his parents own a real-estate company and are constantly out of town, speaking at conventions and getting richer. When they are around, they throw fund-raisers that my parents try to avoid. Their faces are all over billboards and parents'-club newsletters—his mom in her crisp black suits and his dad with his golf clubs and smug grin.

Now SPOILED is tugging at Henry's hair, too. Henry stares straight ahead with an annoyed smirk, but doesn't tell them to stop. I choose a seat across the room from them, up front by the door.

Mr. Robertson starts to take roll.

"Matthew Livingston?"

"Here."

"Valerie Watson?"

"Present!" ANGEL chirps.

"Dylan Schuster?"

It's a name I don't recognize. No one answers. Mr. Robertson looks up.

"No Dylan Schuster?"

The door opens in front of me and a girl pokes her head in. Her face isn't familiar and this school is small enough that everyone looks familiar. Her hair is the darkest brown, almost black, and messy, much messier than the tousled look that a lot of the girls are going for. It makes her look like she's been electrocuted. She has black eyeliner smudged around quick eyes that dart across the room and back again. She looks as though she's deciding whether to come in or stay out.

"Dylan Schuster?" Mr. Robertson asks again.

The new girl looks at him and her eyes widen.

"Wow," she says. "You're good."

He laughs and she strides in, a messenger bag slung over her shoulder, a cup of coffee in her hand. Her thin T-shirt has been torn down one side and safety-pinned back together. Her jeans are the tightest I've ever seen, and she is so tall and so skinny. Her boots *thump*, *thump*, *thump* to the back of the classroom. I don't turn around to watch her, but I picture her choosing the back corner seat. I picture her slouching.

When Mr. Robertson finishes taking roll, he walks up and down the rows of desks, telling us about all the things we'll learn this year.

6

I'm alone in the science building, standing on its green, scuffed-up floors, inhaling the musty air. Taylor and the rest of the popular kids have all probably claimed lockers in the English hall. Last year, Ingrid and I chose ours in the foreign-language building, right next to English, still visible but without as much school spirit. The science hall is no one's first choice. It's out of the way of everything but science classes, completely off the social radar. I wish it could stay empty forever.

It feels wrong to shut a lock around something that only has air inside. I consider waiting until I have something worthy of locking up, but this is a prize: it's the northernmost locker in the northernmost building of Vista High. If I walked out the door now, I would be on the sidewalk. If I crossed the street, I wouldn't be here anymore. And maybe it's the idea of escaping that makes me realize the perfect thing to make this locker my own.

I don't have any tape, so I bite off half a piece of gum and chew it for a second, take it out of my mouth, and stick it to the back of Ingrid's hill photo. The locker has a dulled, scratched-up rectangular mirror inside. I am careful not to make eye contact with myself, but I can't help catching a glimpse of straight brown hair, a few freckles. My face is hazy, narrower than it used to be. I press the picture over the mirror and I'm gone. What's left is this pretty, calm place.

Someone leans against the lockers next to me. Dylan. Her hair is even messier up close. Strands stick out all around her face.

"Hey," she says.

"Hi."

She stares at me for so long that I start to wonder if I look weird, if there's ink on my forehead or something. Then she gives me this smile that's hard to pin down. It's sort of amused, but not in a bad way. Before she leaves, she rummages in the bag she's carrying and slams her lock onto the empty locker next to mine. She stomps away and I'm alone again. I shut the door slowly, listen to the hinges groan. When I close my lock around the handle, it makes a neat, soft click and claim it as mine.

7

I'm just a few steps off campus when Mom pulls over in her Volvo station wagon.

She leans out the window and yells, "Caitlin!" as if I might not have noticed my own mother pulling over, like the car she's been driving all my life and the PEACE IS PATRIOTIC bumper sticker didn't tip me off. I do this awkward skip-walk to the car while all the other kids drive past me to meet up at Starbucks or the mall. I toss my backpack onto the passenger's seat and follow it inside.

"Why aren't you at work?" I ask, slouching so I won't be so conspicuous.

Mom has the most presidential name ever—Margaret Carter-Madison—and even though all she runs is a small elementary school, people are always clamoring for her time. It's amazing the things she has to deal with—parents who are obsessed with their six-year-olds' social development; Mrs. Smith, who's this warped fifth-grade teacher who insists dinosaurs never existed; occasional lice epidemics—sometimes I don't understand how she can handle the pressure of it all. Somehow, though, she always manages to stay calm. She has a voice that's a little quieter than most people's, so you have to pay closer attention when you listen to her, and instead of sitting in the audience during the little kids' productions, trying to look interested, she plays the piano for them. She gets all excited, even though the songs are the same every year.

She's not answering my question, so I say, "I thought if you left Riverbank Elementary before seven P.M. the results would be disastrous."

"Well, it's your first day back," she says, sounding a little too cheerful.

"And that means what exactly?"

"I thought we'd go to our Japanese place. You've just begun the second half of your high school career. We should celebrate."

I get kind of squirmy when she says that. I don't know why she's trying so hard. I mean, *our* Japanese place? We haven't been there since I was a kid. We used to go sometimes back before she became a principal and started working all the time, when I could still order the children's special bento box. I don't know how to respond, so I open up the glove compartment and dig around in it, just for something to do. Tic Tacs. A pair of old sunglasses. The car manual.

I pop a Tic Tac in my mouth and offer her one. She accepts. I keep eating them, one by one, crushing them to minty dust between my teeth. By the time we pull up to the restaurant, I've finished them. I toss the empty see-through box back into the glove compartment before I get out.

It's that slow, in-between time—too late for lunch, too early for dinner. Mom and I are the only customers, which is something I hate. Whenever there are no other customers in a restaurant, I can't stop thinking that if we weren't here, the waiters would probably be eating or talking on the phone or turning the music up, so I feel like we're ruining what should be their downtime. I especially hate it when they hover in a corner, waiting to refill the water glasses. That really depresses me.

The whole time we're looking at our menus, and ordering, and pouring green tea from a hot metal pot into tiny cups, I can feel Mom preparing to say something. I don't know how I know exactly, it's just this feeling I get. She keeps looking at me and smiling.

"Who did you eat lunch with at school?"

I pick up the tiny cup and start to take a sip. Too hot. I set it down and stare at the wet circle it made on the paper place mat.

"Guess," I say.

She doesn't.

I trace the circle with my finger. "Come on. It's obvious."

"Not to me."

I roll my eyes. "*Obviously,* I ate with no one."

Mom's cheery mood disintegrates.

"Caitlin," she says.

She says my name all the time, but this is different. It's all disappointed-sounding, like I had a choice, like there were a million kids lined up to eat with me and I was like, *Sorry, I'd rather eat by myself.*

"What?" I snap, and she doesn't say anything else.

After about two seconds of waiting, the waiter comes with our food. I stare into the enormous bento box I ordered, heaped with tempura and chicken teriyaki and California rolls, and part of me wishes I could still get the kids' box. It has everything that this one does, just smaller portions. I eat one tempura carrot, and feel full.

"My friend Margie at work suggested a very good therapist. Her daughter enjoys working with her."

"What's wrong with Margie's daughter?"

"Nothing is wrong with her. Like you, she's just going through a difficult time right now."

"Oh," I say, all sarcastic. "A *difficult time*."

Mom sips her tea. I bite into a California roll and soy sauce dribbles down my chin. I swat it away with my napkin and hope the waiter isn't standing somewhere watching us.

"I'm not going to see some therapist," I mutter.

Mom looks, sadly, into her rice bowl. I wish I knew what she was thinking.

We don't say much after that, and I feel kind of bad about it, but I don't know why she had to bring that up. She can't expect me to go along with every suggestion she makes just because she's taking me out to eat.

8

Friday-night dinner, I sit at the table with Mom and Dad and eat in silence. Dad asks questions about my first week back at school in the cheerful tone Mom has been using for days. I give him one-word answers, stab pasta with my fork. Soon they start talking to each other and I tune them out. When I can't sit there any longer I get up, push the leftover food into the sink, and stick my plate in the dishwasher.

I climb into the backseat of my car and put my knees up against the seat covers I ruined. I was supposed to have gotten my license three months ago, but instead of making three-point turns, I was watching my best friend's casket lower into the ground. Now I can't seem to call the DMV to schedule a new appointment.

This car is so old it only has a tape player. I only own one tape. Fortunately, it's a good one. Ingrid's brother, Davey, made it for my birthday one year. It has all these indie bands on it that I had never heard of. The songs kind of blend together, but they're all so great. I reach up, turn the key in the ignition, and a boy's voice wails through the speakers. A few minutes later my dad comes out to the car.

"Do you have any homework? If you get it done now, you'll be able to enjoy the weekend."

"No," I lie.

He lifts my backpack into the air. "I brought you this just in case."

After a while I pull out my math book and some paper. The tape turns itself over. There's the sound of a quiet guitar; a woman's voice starts and then a man's joins her. It sounds pretty. I try to do my math, but I don't have a calculator in the car. All of a sudden I want the phone to ring. I picture my mom coming out with the cordless and handing it to me when I roll the window down. I would stretch out on the seat. And listen. And talk. I would come up with something interesting to say. But the only person who ever called me was Ingrid, so I know it will never happen. I reach up and turn the music as loud as it can go. The whole car shakes and it sounds like I'm tuned to a radio station that doesn't come in clearly.

I push everything off the backseat and lie down. Through the moon roof, the sky darkens. I imagine that the phone is propped on the seat, right next to my ear.

So what was Veena wearing the first day? Ingrid asks.

I didn't notice.

Of course you noticed. I bet it was something new.

She acted like she didn't know me. I wasn't exactly paying attention to her clothes.

Imagine her cleaning out her cat's litter box.

Did you hear what I said? All week long, she acted like she hates me.

Oh my God, I know: imagine her finding moldy leftovers in her refrigerator.

I don't feel like it.

How was it without me? Did you hide out in the library at lunch with all the nerds?

Actually, I ate with Alicia McIntosh. She brought me a tank top that said CHARITY and told me that if I promised to wear it every day she would let me follow her around and stand in the cafeteria line to buy her Diet Cokes.

Did you miss me?

Why are you asking?

I want to know.

It's obvious.

I want to hear you say it. It'll make me feel good.

Fuck you.

Come on. Just say it.

Mom appears right outside my window. She waves at me from six inches away. I don't move. She points at her watch, which means that it's late and she wants me inside. I don't sit up. I just close my eyes, wish her away from the car. I'm not ready.

Wailing Boy is back on—I've been in here for ninety minutes—and I squeeze my eyes shut tighter and listen to him. His guitar gets urgent, his voice trembles. I can feel it: his heart is broken.

9

The next morning, my dad knocks on my car window to wake me up. I snuck back out in the middle of the night and slept here.

"I have a surprise for you," he says, beaming, voice muffled by the glass. "It's around the side."

"What is it?" I'm so tired I can hardly talk.

"Come see," he says, real singsongy.

I unlock my door and step out into the daylight. I need to brush my teeth.

Dad covers my eyes with his hand and leads me around to the other side of my car. Beneath my thin slipper soles, I can feel the pebbles of the driveway, the stepping-stones that run through the grass alongside the house, and, finally, the grass itself. We're in the backyard. Our actual house isn't anything special. Like most of the houses in Los Cerros, it's big and new and plain, but I love our yard. There's a path that weaves around all the vegetables and flowers and on the weekends my parents spend hours out here in the dirt, gardening. The best part is that if you stand on the path and look away from the house, you can't even see where the yard ends. It stretches on and on for acres. It's hilly and there are a bunch of ancient oak trees.

He uncovers my eyes, and sweeps his arm out toward a huge pile of wood lying on the brick patio that separates the house from the garden. It's cut in thick planks that are at least ten feet long. Dad's standing there in front of the gigantic messy pile, smiling all proud like he just bought me a beach house in Fiji and a private jet to get me there.

"Wood," I say, confused.

"It's all sanded already. I got you a top-of-the-line saw, too. That should be coming on Monday."

"What am I supposed to do with it?"

He shrugs. "I have no idea," he says. "You're the expert."

My parents have this crazy idea that I'm good at building things just because once I went to this arts-and-crafts summer camp and made a little wooden stepladder that actually turned out okay.

"That was like a million years ago," I remind my dad. "I was twelve."

"I'm sure you'll get the hang of it again soon."

"This is a lot of wood."

"There's plenty more when you need it. I don't want you to feel limited."

All I can do is nod my head up and down, up and down. I mean, I know what's going on. I hear my parents talking about me, sounding all worried. I know that this is supposed to be some alternative to therapy. Dad thinks it's a really great gift that will take my mind off my screwed-up life.

He stands there, looking hopeful, waiting for me to react. Finally,

I walk over to the pile and run my fingers across a piece on the top. I knock on it with my knuckles. I can feel him watching me. I look up and force a smile.

"Great," he says, all final, like something has been decided.

"Yeah," I say back, like I understand.

10

The first day Ingrid and I ditched was gray and cold. We left at lunch and I was sure someone would catch us, but no one did.

Once we were safely out of view, we started walking up this hill to where the condos are all jammed up against one another; windows look into neighbors' living rooms. It was so quiet.

The diner or the mall? Ingrid asked.

Too many people at the mall. I kicked at some rocks on the path and watched the dust rise.

When we got to the top of the hill, Ingrid ran into the middle of an empty street. She turned to face me, wavy hair blown across her face, arms lifted until they stuck straight out at her sides. She started twirling. Her red skirt billowed. The wind blew harder and she spun so fast she was a blur. When she stopped she crouched over.

Oh my God. She laughed. *Oh my God, my head.*

She tried to walk back over to me, stumbled, and laughed harder.

You're such a nerd, I said.

A middle-aged woman came toward us from between two condos and my stomach tightened. But she just walked by us, didn't even say anything. We were at the top of this hill and we didn't have anywhere to go.

I turned around. *Look,* I said.

Below us was our school, a collection of rectangular boxes. Even though we knew that the kids were studying for tests and kissing and worrying about one another, in that moment they were so small—only colorful specks moving around.

This feels good, Ingrid said.

The day was gloomy, so I got this idea. I said, *I bet there's no one at the park.* And I was right. When we got there, the field where little kids usually ran around was empty. No one was sliding on the slide or dangling from the monkey bars. We made sure that there wasn't anyone at the sandbox and then Ingrid put her hands on my shoulders. *You, my friend,* she said, *are a genius.*

She ran over to the swings and I followed her. I sat on the rubber seat, and started to pump really hard with my legs. We were both going so high, moving through the air together, shouting our conversation because of the wind and because we didn't have to worry about anyone listening. We got so high that I thought any second one of us might go all the way around. Ingrid had her camera around her neck and she clutched it to her chest with one arm so it wouldn't fly off.

The clouds were low and heavy and dark. Then the sky turned this bright gray and it started to rain.

Ingrid snapped a photograph of me swinging before she tucked the camera under her jacket, but if she ever developed it, she never showed it to me.

Soon it was pouring. The cold felt good, and we kept swinging until our hair and our clothes were drenched, laughing, talking about something that I can never remember, even though I try.

ll

Ms. Delani stands in front of us, her smile tight across her face.

"Today," she says. "I'm going to hold short conferences with each of you to establish your personal artistic goals for the semester."

She scans the room, probably wondering if any of us are worth her precious time. In her other life, she's a real artist. Once Ingrid and I went to this tiny gallery in the city for one of her openings. We were the only students who showed up—she hadn't mentioned it to many people. Everyone there was dressed up, and there were a couple bottles of champagne and a platter of grapes and some Brie. We had spent the whole BART ride trying to predict what her art would be like.

When she caught sight of us in the gallery, she touched the arm of the man she'd been talking to and came up to us. She gave us these quick, firm hugs, so casually, like she'd hugged us a million times before. She introduced us as two of her most promising students, and Ingrid and I showed off for her, dropping names of the famous photographers she had taught in class. All her photographs were of the same things: doll parts scattered over brightly colored fabric. Porcelain arms and legs and middles, but mostly heads. I don't know what I had been expecting, but I hadn't been expecting that. They were beautiful, but kind of unsettling at the same time.

After being there and seeing her drink champagne and talk with this low voice to a bunch of impressed people, I could just feel how lame we all must have seemed to her. All of us except Ingrid, who was actually talented. Like last year, we had an assignment to photograph something that was meaningful to us. I guess she expected us to turn in pictures of really profound things—I can't even think of what—because when she started coming by our desks to see what we came up with and saw a jock's picture of his baseball glove lying on the grass, and a girl's pom-pom against the gym floor, she just about lost it. That smile vanished. She walked back to her desk and put her head in her hands and didn't speak for the rest of the class.

She looks more optimistic today, calling kids over to her desk, one by one. I'm in the far right corner, alone, of course. She starts with Akiko, who is sitting in the front left of the room. I assume that she hopes she'll run out of time before my turn comes. I lay my head on my desk and shut my eyes.

Forty minutes later I wake up.

Everything is muffled, but it only seems like that because I'm disoriented and kind of embarrassed that I actually fell asleep.

When I lift my head and see that nothing new is happening, that everyone is still sitting together at their tables and Ms. Delani is meeting with Matt, I just close my eyes again and listen to people talking. Meghan and Katie are writing notes to each other and whispering, *Oh my God!* and *No he did not!* Dustin and James are talking in low voices about some new skate park.

I hear Katie saying, all importantly, "Henry's mom is the real estate agent who was showing the house they bought, and she told Henry that the family was nice but just not the kind of people who belong in our community."

"I heard she's a *lesbian*," Meghan says. To judge by her tone, she might as well be saying, *I hear she digs garbage from trash cans and eats it.*

"I heard that, too," Lulu whispers. "I heard she got kicked out of her old school for making out with a girl in the bathroom."

I realize they're talking about Dylan, and for some reason it really pisses me off.

"Excuse me, but some of us are trying to sleep," I say, glaring at them.

They look at me, then at each other. They stop talking for a moment. Meghan runs her hand down one side of her neatly combed brown hair. Katie buttons a pearl button on her sweater. They look like miniatures of their mothers.

"Caitlin?" Ms. Delani says. She's scanning the classroom, like she called my name off a random list and she doesn't know who I am.

"I'm over here," I tell her.

"Will you come to my desk, please?"

I look at the clock. There aren't even two minutes left.

I get up and walk to her desk. She has a folder of my photographs from last year and she's looking at them through her little glasses. She sighs, tucks some of her straight black hair behind her ear.

"You definitely need to work on your use of color this semester. Look at this one," she says, but I don't.

I look straight at her face. She doesn't even notice.

"Do you see how there is no contrast here? If we were to convert this image to black-and-white, you would see that all these colors would be the same value of gray. It has a dulling effect."

I keep looking at her and she keeps looking at my photo. Last year she wasn't like this. She may have paid more attention to Ingrid, but she talked to me, too.

She sifts through the stack. "Your compositions are sometimes good, but . . ." She shakes her head. "Even they need quite a bit of work."

I want to say, *Fuck you*, Veena. *They were obviously okay with you last year, because you gave me an A.* But I don't say anything. I'm just waiting for her to look up at me so she can see me glaring. The bell rings. She looks up at the clock, back at the stack, and says, "Okay?"

"Okay, what?"

"I'll see you tomorrow."

I shake my head.

"But what are my goals?" I ask. I just want her to look at me.

"Color," she says, staring at my pictures. "Composition."

I'm about to ask her what she means, how I can just get better, where I should start. But she's already turned and walking to her back office. The door shuts.

12

I'm headed up to the science building, holding a cold slice of greasy pizza. On my way through the quad I see Jayson Michaels. There are only a few black kids at our school, so he stands out. Plus he's really popular—track star, runs the mile in 4:20 flat. We went to the same junior high and had homeroom together in sixth grade, and the only thing that I really remember about it was that when we were discussing segregation the teacher randomly asked Jayson how he felt about it. She asked him right there in the middle of everyone. As if a sixth grader who had lived his whole life in this practically all-white town would feel like being a spokesperson for Black America. And anyway, what a dumb question. What's he gonna say? *Well, actually, I feel pretty good about it. It's pretty uplifting that people like me couldn't get served in restaurants or use public bathrooms.*

Now he takes a step toward me. I haven't seen him this close for years. His eyes are lighter brown than I remember. His face is smooth and he has a nick on his right cheek, at the jaw.

I can't remember a single thing that Jayson and I ever said to each other. Still, I know these personal things about him because he told Ingrid and she told me. Like he has a sister who's in college, who he talks to on the phone a lot. And he lives with his dad alone. He loves to run because it makes him forget about everything else. When he trains, he listens to old groups like the Jackson Five.

Now he looks at me like he knows me.

And I get this feeling. It's like my head suddenly gets lighter, fills up with air. I want to talk. Jayson opens his mouth. Then he closes it. Then he opens it again.

"Hi," he says.

It's the saddest *hi* I've ever heard.

We hesitate, but it only lasts a moment.

Then we keep walking, away from each other.

13

It's the weekend again, and even though I know I should be building something with the wood that's been waiting in the backyard all week, all I want to do is lie on my bed and listen to music. I keep getting these songs in my head that I want to put on, but I have to get up to change tracks because I can't find the remote to my stereo. After I've done this about twenty times, I finally decide to just look for it. It isn't buried under the covers. It isn't under all the clothes piled on top of my chest of drawers, or sitting on top of my CDs or my desk. I get down on the carpet to look under my bed. I stick my arm under and feel around, find a couple mismatched socks, a progress report from school that I hid from my parents last year, and something I don't recognize—hard and flat and dusty. I pull it out, thinking maybe it's a yearbook from elementary school, and then I see it and my heart stops. Worn pages, bird painted on the blue cover in Wite-Out.

Ingrid's journal.

For some reason, I feel afraid. It's like I'm split down the middle and one half of me wants to open it more than I've ever wanted to do anything. The other half is so scared. I can't stop shaking.

Did it get kicked under the bed one night by accident?

Did she hide it?

She carried it with her everywhere. I know this sounds stupid, but I felt kind of jealous of it. Whenever I had to figure something out or vent, I would just call her up, so I couldn't understand why she needed to have this book that was so private. But here it is, in my hands, and I'm holding it like it's some alive thing.

I stare at it in my hands forever, just feeling its weight, looking at the place where one Wite-Out wing is starting to flake off. Then, once my hands are steadied, I open to the first page. It's a drawing of her face—yellow hair; blue eyes; small, crooked smile. She's looking straight ahead. Birds fly across the background. She drew them blurry, to show movement, and across the top she wrote, *Me on a Sunday Morning.*

I turn the page.

As I read, I can hear Ingrid's voice, hushed and fast, like she's telling me secrets.

DEAR HALL MONITOR,

go ahead. call my parents, send me to detention, make me clean up trash at lunch. i didn't go to bio today. it couldn't be helped. i was already feeling so nervous, heart pounding a billion times a minute for no reason except that just thinking about sitting next to jayson made me want to puke. even though it's the only like thing i ever look forward to. crushes are supposed to be fun, aren't they? they definitely aren't supposed to be so torturous. i passed him at his locker in the english hall on my way to meet caitlin and he smiled at me and my stomach cramped up. i told caitlin 'we have to leave' even though i knew that her fifth period class is the only one she likes because mr. harris is the coolest teacher i've never had. she could tell that i meant it, though, because she got her serious face on and just left with me. that's why i love her so much. that's why i wish i was a better person. maybe you'll spare me this once. you have a nice face and a shit job. maybe your life is hard and maybe you've just waiting for a kid to listen to you complain about it. if you don't call my parents i promise i won't call you 'nails' like the other kids do because i'll know that you aren't hard like them at all, and i'll slow down when i pass you in the hallways just in case you decide that then's the time to talk.

love,
ingrid

I shut the book.

My room is so quiet and empty it hurts.

I know I should want to keep reading but I can't. It's too much. I put her journal in my chest of drawers, not in the top drawer where everyone puts things they want to hide, but buried in clothes all the way at the back of a drawer near the bottom. But after a few minutes I move it. That place doesn't seem right. So I put it on a shelf in the walk-in closet I painted purple a couple summers ago. I slide a shoe box full of photo negatives in front of it.

I stand in the doorway of my closet and look in at the shelf. I almost expect to see the shoe box rising and falling with the journal's breath. But it's just a journal. It isn't alive. Something is wrong with me.

An hour later I reach up and touch it to make sure it's still there.

After lunch I move it again. This time, I put it back under my bed, because that's where it's been for the past three months. I try to do homework. I try to watch TV. But all I can think about is Ingrid's journal, in my room, and if it's still there, and what if someone finds it, and why I don't want to read it, and how I know I need to.

The next morning, already dressed, shoes tied, hair pulled back in my perpetual ponytail, I stand in front of the closet again. I want to walk out the door but I can't. I don't mean *I can't* like *I don't want to.* I mean, *I can't,* like something is physically making it impossible for me to leave my room without it. So I crouch over my backpack and find an inside zipper pocket. The pocket's pretty small, so I don't know if it will work, but I take Ingrid's journal from the shelf and try to fit it in, and it turns out to be perfect. It rests there, hidden.

I close my backpack and heave it over one shoulder, then the other. The journal makes it so much heavier, but the weight feels good.

14

On Mr. Robertson's stereo, John Lennon and Paul McCartney are singing the word *love* over and over. He lowers the volume to let the song fade out, pushes the sleeves of his worn-in beige sweater up to his elbows.

"When I was a kid, my parents used to play 'All You Need Is Love' on our record player almost every night," he says, perched on his desk, looking out at us. "At the time I thought it was just something to dance around to. I memorized the lyrics before I even considered what they meant. It was just fun to sing along." He reaches for a stack of papers next to him, and walks in between the rows of desks, handing the papers out to us. "But if you look here at the lyrics, you'll see that it has many elements of a poem."

He sets my copy on my table and I look at his wedding band and the little hairs below his knuckles. I wonder what his wife is like, and if they dance around their house at night listening to the Beatles or other old bands. I try to imagine their house, how they have it decorated, and I think they probably have lots of plants, and real paintings on the wall painted by people they're friends with.

"Caitlin." Mr. Robertson smiles at me, interrupts my thoughts. "Show us one poetic element in this song."

"Okay," I say. I read it over quickly, but I'm so worried about taking forever to answer that I don't really absorb anything. "If you look at it," I say, "you'll see that there is a . . . pattern? Things repeat a lot?"

"Great. Repetition. Benjamin, what else?"

"Uh, like a theme?"

"Of what?"

"Love, I guess."

"Okay. What's another theme of this song? Dylan?"

I glance at her and wonder if she really got kicked out of her old school for making out with a girl. She's wearing the same black jeans, but today with a light blue shirt with some words on it that I can't read. She has bulky leather bracelets on each wrist and she's sitting with one elbow on the desk, holding her handout in front of her face.

"Human potential. Or identity," she mutters.

"Great," Mr. Robinson says. He nods. "Wonderful." He looks at one corner of the ceiling and hums a little bit of the song. He seems to forget where he is for a minute.

Then he returns to us.

He says, "For homework, please choose a song that matters to you. I want you to write a paper that first explains why the song is important to your life, and then analyzes the song's lyrics as you would a poem. I'll give you until Friday."

I'm getting my math book from my locker when Dylan comes up next to me and asks, "Is there anywhere good to eat around here?"

By now, the secret is out—almost all the lockers in the science hall have been claimed. Before school and after school, the hall echoes with locker doors groaning open and slamming shut, with forty people's voices and ringing cell phones and stomping feet. When I glance at Dylan, she's staring like she did the first day. Her eyes are this clear blue green, surrounded by black smudged makeup. She's standing close to me, and it feels strange. Apart from being accosted by Alicia, I haven't been letting people get near me.

"If you go down Webster," I say, "toward downtown, there are a few places."

She looks at Ingrid's hill stuck to the door of my locker, cocks her head, and squints at it. Then she nods her approval.

"So," she says, "hungry?"

Without thinking, without even considering going, I say, "I have homework."

"Okay," she says. "Whatever."

I head home, ready to pull Ingrid's journal out of my backpack as soon as I get there and read for hours, until I've finished every entry. But as I pass the hills and the condos and all the places we used to walk past together, I decide that isn't something I should do.

Here's how I feel: People take one another for granted. Like, I'd hang out with Ingrid in all of these random places—in her room or at school or just on some sidewalk somewhere. And the whole time we'd tell each other things, just say all of our thoughts out loud. Maybe that would've been boring to some people, but it was never boring to us. I never realized what a big deal that was. How amazing it is to find someone who wants to hear about all the things that go on in your head. You just think that things will stay the way they are. You never look up, in a moment that feels like every other moment of your life, and think, *Soon this will be over.* But I understand more now. About the way life works. I know that when I finish reading Ingrid's journal, there won't be anything new between us ever again.

So when I get back to my house, I lock my room door even though I'm the only one home, take Ingrid's journal out, and just hold it for a little while. I look at the drawing on the first page again. And then I put the journal back. I'm going to try to make her last.

15

After dinner, I climb into the backseat of my car with my laptop. I push in Davey's mix tape, but I keep the volume low so I can concentrate. I'm thinking of ways to start my English paper.

I type, *Music is a powerful way for people to express themselves.* Then I delete it. I try again: *Songs can be important ways of remembering certain moments in people's lives.* That's closer to what I'm trying to say, but it isn't exactly right yet. I shut my computer. A girl plays her guitar, sings earnestly, and I crank open the moon roof, sink lower on the seat, look up at the sky, and listen.

When the song is over, I turn the tape off, and try again. *There is an indescribable feeling that comes from being desperately in love with a song.*

I read the sentence over. I keep writing, trying to feel the best night of my life over again.

Ingrid and I had stood in front of her bathroom mirror, concentrating. The counter was cluttered with little makeup containers and bobby pins and hair goop.

We are so hot, Ingrid said.

I nodded, slowly, watching my face as it moved up and down. My hair was shiny and straight and long, parted down the middle. Ingrid had put this deep green, glittery eye shadow on me and it made my eyes look amber instead of just brown. She had pinned her blond curls back messily, and was wearing red lipstick that made her look older and kind of sophisticated.

Yeah, I said. *We look really good.*

We look amazing.

What it was, was that we complemented each other. We just fit in this way that made strangers ask us if we were sisters, even though her hair was blond and curly and mine was straight and dark. Even though her eyes were blue and mine were brown. Maybe it was the way we acted, or spoke, or just *moved.* The way we would look at something and both have the same thought at the same moment, and turn to each other at the same time and start to say the same thing.

Okay, Ingrid said. *Hold still.* She put pink lip gloss on my mouth with this little wand thing, and I licked my finger and wiped off a speck of mascara that had gotten on her cheek.

We climbed into the back of Ingrid's parents' SUV, and Ingrid's mom, Susan, looked at our reflection in the rearview mirror.

You two look great, she said. In the mirror, I could see that she was smiling. Mitch, Ingrid's dad, turned in his seat to see us.

Look at you two. What a sight. Which I think was his way of saying he thought we looked good, too.

Ingrid's brother, Davey, and his girlfriend, Amanda, had just gotten engaged, and they were throwing a huge party at a restaurant near their apartment to celebrate. Ingrid's parents had Davey ten years before they had her. She always liked to say that she was a mistake, but Susan and Mitch never admitted it. All the people at the party would be older, but that didn't matter. We still got to dress up and look forward to something. We still got to get out of Los Cerros for a night.

Mitch and Susan dropped us off in front so that we wouldn't have to drive around with them, searching for parking for an hour. We found Davey and Amanda inside the restaurant, smiling and looking so happy like they always did.

After we had talked with them for a while, we found a table and ate all these small dishes of fancy food. The lights dimmed and the music got louder, and everyone got up and started to dance. All of Amanda and Davey's friends were beautiful, but for once I felt beautiful, too. I got up and walked out into the middle of them, wearing my black V-neck sweater and the tight maroon pants I got from the mall. Ingrid followed me in her yellow dress and brown boots. It felt good to be in the middle of strangers. I didn't feel like a kid in high school. I was anyone I wanted to be.

We started dancing, real jumpy and twirly, to these British rock bands we hadn't heard before. At one point we danced our way back over to the edge of all the people, and a waiter came by with a tray of champagne. Ingrid grabbed two glasses before he could take a good look at her, and we drank them down fast. It didn't make me drunk, exactly, I mean it was only *one* glass, but it did make me feel a little bit dizzy, and that made the dancing even more fun. And then, after we had danced through about five songs straight, a new song started, and as soon as the man started singing, with this voice that was urgent and calm and passionate all at once, I froze. I stood in the middle of all the dancing strangers and I just listened.

It was the moment I realized what music can do to people, how it can make you hurt and feel so good all at once. I just stood there with my eyes closed, feeling the movement of all the people around me, the vibration of the bass rise through the floor to my throat, while something inside me broke and came back together.

When the song was over I grabbed Ingrid's hand and pulled her out of the crowd, over to Amanda, who was standing with the DJ, handing him CDs and telling him which tracks to play. These huge speakers were next to them and I could feel the bass pounding through me.

What band was that? I shouted.

The Cure, Amanda shouted back. *Like them?*

I nodded. I wanted to say, *I* love *them,* but the word felt too simple.

Amanda put the CD back in its case and handed it to me. *Take it,* she said. *It's yours.*

A couple hours later my paper is finished. Through my car window, I can see the lights are all off in the house. My parents must be sleeping already. I guess they're used to me being out here now. I cross the path toward the house, stop at the pile of wood. I run my hands along a plank at the top.

16

I wake up before my alarm this morning, roll over, and shut it off. It took forever to fall asleep. I kept thinking about that night. After that were months that Ingrid was alive but not really awake. She would still draw in her journal and hang out with me and laugh sometimes and everything, but now, looking back, I know that she did it all automatically. The way you brush your teeth and eat breakfast. You don't really think about it; your mind is other places. It's just something you do to get ready for something else.

I pull out Ingrid's journal, and I'm pretty sure that I deserve to, seeing as it's only six forty-five and already a bad day. But when I open it everything just gets worse.

Dear Veena,

this is a thank you letter. yesterday i carried my camera around with me and just took all of these pictures — i saw everything different, everything was cropped into rectangular boxes and my eyes were taking pictures before my camera was. and then i got them developed at the one hour place where this scruffy cute boy flirted with me and said 'yer photos are really great' and i was just happy and really eager to see them so i just said thanks and i wasn't like 'that was totally illegal for you to just look at my pictures like that.' and they are really good especially the flower ones and the one of the broken glass and concrete and oh yeah also the one of me reflected in the window of the record store with all the disgusting teen girl singer posters with fake breasts that are way too big for their skinny stick bodies and there i am reflected a real girl with my camera. veena, because of you my life might actually turn out OK. i'll get wild and travel all over the world and take photos of animals and tribal people and get hired by national geographic and have all of these amazing adventures and wild sex with gorgeous men who speak only some very rare dialect so we'll only communicate with body language and therefore never stay in touch. or i'll give my parents heart attacks and go to some new york art school instead of real college and become famous for my pictures that capture the souls of hookers and heroin addicts and runaway kids who live on sidewalks and sleep in flophouses and when i give my acceptance speech after i win the nobel peace prize i will say 'really it all started with you, veena delani. i owe it all to you.' and you'll be all teary and proud.

LOVE,
INGRID

17

Obviously, I skip photo this morning.

I sit on the path behind the apartments, pathetically alone, and wait for 8:50 to come. I turn my back to the buildings and look at the hill and the trees. I start to count the trees. Then, without really realizing it, I start to think of one thing I did wrong for each tree I look at. Wide oak—I didn't tell anyone when Ingrid cut herself. Baby oak—the time I told her I was getting sick of hearing about Jayson's arms and his blue shirt. Tall tree with bare branches—the way I would leave when she got depressed and stopped talking. I should have stayed. I should have just sat quietly, so that she knew I was with her. Pine tree—the afternoon I lied and said that I didn't feel like hanging out with her every single day, when really I just didn't want to steal nail polish from Long's because I felt so shitty the one time we did it. I could tell she was about to cry, even though she turned around and left. That was the day she got caught with eyeliner and hair dye stuffed into her backpack. I pick out a smaller pine for not being there to get caught with her. Then I look out to where there's this huge group of trees in the distance, and I count those for all the times I called her some name, or told her she was being stupid—because even though I was always joking, it might have hurt.

The morning fog spreads from tree to tree like a blanket of regret. I take my camera out of my backpack. I want so badly to take a picture. But I don't.

18

I walk into my precalc class and surprise myself by sliding into the seat behind Taylor.

"She slit her wrists," I say.

Taylor turns around to face me. He looks uncertain, the way he does when he can't find the value of x. I make sure to lock eyes with him. Anger is tying knots in my stomach.

"What?" he asks.

"Slit her wrists, bled to death. That's how she did it. Usually it doesn't work, I guess, but she meant it."

He looks uncomfortable, pale. His eyes dart away from mine.

"Now you know," I say.

I lean back in the chair, away from him. Mr. James reviews the homework on his ancient overhead projector, but I can't concentrate. I just see her. I blink hard, then stare at the desk, hoping the blankness will push the image away. Someone has written YOU SUCK in ugly black marker on the top right corner. I rub the letters so hard that my thumb cramps. The words don't get any lighter. I'm breathing hard and I think Taylor turns to face me again, but I choose not to look.

"I have to change desks," I mutter to no one, and grab my backpack and walk down the aisle until I find a desk with a clear surface, no marks.

But I still see her as if I were there in her house that morning. Like it was me instead of her mom who pushed Ingrid's bathroom door open and saw her naked in the bathtub, eyes shut, head heavy, arms floating in that red water. I look up at Mr. James's projector, but what I see are the gashes in her arms, along the veins. I can't hear what he is saying. First the sounds go away and then everything loses shape.

Slowly, slowly, I lower my head until my face is flat against the cold desktop. I concentrate on breathing, feel my heart working hard. I can hear the clock faintly ticking. I look to the wall, to the spot where I know it is, and through the buzz of Mr. James's voice, I wait for it to come back in focus.

19

Ingrid's skin was the smoothest texture, so pale that it was transparent. I could see the blue veins that ran down her arms, and they made her seem fragile somehow. The way Eric Daniels, my first boyfriend, seemed fragile when I laid my head on his chest and heard his heart beating and thought, *Oh.* People don't always remember about the blood and the heartbeat. The lungs. But whenever I looked at Ingrid, I was reminded of the things that kept her alive.

The first time she carved something into her skin, she used the sharp tip of an X-Acto knife. She lifted her shirt up to show me after the cuts had scabbed over. She had scrawled FUCK YOU on her stomach. I stood quiet for a moment, feeling the breath get knocked out of me. I should have grabbed her arm and taken her straight to the nurse's office, into that small room with two cots covered in paper sheets and the sweet, stale medicine smell.

I should have lifted Ingrid's shirt to show the cuts. *Look,* I would've said to the nurse at her little desk, eyeglasses perched on her pointed nose. *Help her.*

Instead, I reached my hand out and traced the words. The cuts were shallow, so the scabs only stood out a little bit. They were rough and brown. I knew that a lot of girls at our school cut themselves. They wore their long sleeves pulled down past their wrists and made slits for their thumbs so that the scars on their arms wouldn't show. I wanted to ask Ingrid if it hurt to do that to herself, but I felt stupid, like I must have been missing something, so what I said was, *Fuck you, too, Bitch.* Ingrid giggled, and I tried to ignore the feeling that something good between us was changing.

20

Dad greets me at the bottom of the stairs, dangling my favorite pair of sneakers by their laces.

"Look at these," he commands. "These are shocking."

He shows me the bottoms, where the rubber is almost worn through. Shaking his head, he says, "People will think we deprive you. They'll call Child Protection on us. We need to find you new shoes ASAP."

I roll my eyes at him. It's Saturday morning, and he's wearing a polo with the most hideous shorts in history. I glance down at his shoes. Unfortunately, they are spotless.

"Fine," I say.

I trudge upstairs and look in my mirror, rub some cover-up under my eyes so that I don't look too terrible to go out into the world, heave my backpack over my shoulders, and meet him back downstairs.

"You don't really need that, do you?" he asks, pointing to my backpack.

"My wallet's in it," I say.

"I'll buy you shoes," he says. "You don't need your wallet."

I'm not leaving her journal behind. "Well, I have, like, *all* my stuff in here. I might need something."

He shrugs. "Suit yourself."

In the car he asks me how the brainstorming is coming.

"Brainstorming?"

"What are you thinking of building?"

"Oh." I look down at the black leather seats and trace my finger along a seam. "I'm still deciding." I try to sound like I have some ideas and I'm just not sure which one to go with yet.

He nods. "Well," he says, "I can't wait to see it, whatever it is."

I don't say anything back and soon he turns the radio on. We listen to two mechanics with thick Boston accents joke around and give car advice.

"Are you thinking of getting your license soon?" my dad asks.

I shrug and look out the window. Everywhere is brightness and I want to shut my eyes.

He glances at me. The mechanics on the radio chuckle. After a while my dad pats my knee.

"No hurry," he says. "You can take your time."

Not too long ago I would have been happy to go shopping, but when we get to the department store it's just too much—all these racks of shoes, all this *stuff* that I'm supposed to want. People are swarming around me, moving from pair to pair, saying, "Oh, how cute," picking up shoes and turning them over to look at the price tag. I just stand here, wondering where to start, forgetting what the point of anything is. I can feel my dad looking at me. I can tell that he wants me to do something, but I can't.

Finally, he picks up a pair of green Converse displayed on a round table in front of us.

"What do you think?" he asks.

"They're nice," I say. And I think of Ingrid's red ones, and how she would write things on the white rubber tips and along the sides.

"We'll take these," my dad says to a salesman. "Size eight. Right, Caitlin?"

I nod.

"Don't you want to try them on?" the salesman asks.

"She'll return them if they don't fit," my dad says, and hands him his credit card.

While we're waiting for the salesman to ring us up, I see this girl from school. I don't know her, I don't even know what her name is. She's in a special program, not the one for the kids with learning disabilities, but the one for what the counselors like to call "at-risk youth." We catch eyes over a display of boots.

"Hey, you go to Vista, right?" she says.

"Yeah."

Her hair is dyed a million shades of brown or blond. It looks like she changes the color every couple days and now her hair is rebelling—blond around her ears, light brown at the roots, orange peeking out on the sides.

"Your name's Caitlin, right? I'm Melanie. You might not know me because I don't walk around campus that much. I eat lunch on the baseball bleachers with some people. It's kind of out of the way, you know?" She says this really fast and nervous.

"I recognize you," I say. I want to ask her how she knows my name, but I think that I already know why, and I don't want to make her explain it. My dad walks up to the cash register to sign the credit-card slip. Melanie's not looking at me. Instead, she's picking up all the boots on the table and turning them over to see the price stickers. The weird thing is that she's hardly looking at the boots themselves. I'm not even sure that she's reading the prices until she winces at one and says, "Ouch."

"Three hundred dollars," she mouths as she drops it back on the table. I'm not sure if she's saying it to me, or to the boot, or to the display in general.

I try to picture myself hanging out with this girl and the rest of her anonymous friends, removed from the rest of the people at school. Maybe it would be easier.

Dad comes back carrying a bag with my new shoes.

"Bye," I say to Melanie.

She lifts a hand and wiggles her fingers at me, but doesn't look in my direction.

Leaving the mall, Dad asks, "Do you know her?" He says it a little too loudly, too casually. My parents are pretty open-minded as far as parents go, but I can tell Dad's a little worried. I'll put it this way: you don't need to know that Melanie's in the "at risk" program to know that something's not quite right with her.

"No," I say. "She's just some girl from school."

21

On Monday morning I get to campus early enough to stop by my locker. As I put my math book onto to the top shelf, I get an impulse to unstick Ingrid's hill for a minute and look in the mirror. All I've been doing in the mornings is showering and throwing

on jeans and old T-shirts. Most of the time the bathroom mirror
is all fogged up by the time I get out of the shower, so I don't even
catch my reflection. I look at the white shirt I'm wearing today and
realize that it might actually be my dad's. It's so big it billows out
around me. I wonder what Ingrid would say if she knew how I've
been letting myself go. *You're not serious about leaving the house in
that?* Or maybe, *Lady! Pull yourself together!* I touch the edge of her
picture and decide not to risk looking.

Thumping comes from down the hallway, and when I glance
away from the hill, Dylan's right next to me, finding the combination on her lock.

"Hey," I say, trying to make up for being so rude on Friday.

Wearily she lifts a hand in greeting and mumbles something in
a language I'm not positive is English.

"Excuse me?"

She points to the silver thermos in her other hand.

"Too early," she slurs. "Haven't finished coffee yet."

When I step into the photo room, the first thing I see is a list
on the chalkboard of people with missing work. There are a few
names up there followed with one or two missing assignments. My
name is the only one followed by *All.*

I think of all the photographs I've wanted to take and it hurts. It
feels awful. But giving Ms. Delani work that I actually care about
would be like inviting her to tear me apart. No thank you. I slump
in my back-row chair, half listening to her explain our next assignment: a still life. She passes her books around to show us examples.
I study the inanimate things. A bowl of fruit. A stack of books. A
pair of dramatically lit, worn-in dancing shoes.

Out of nowhere, inspiration strikes.

I can hardly wait for lunch. When it finally comes, I spot the
hall monitor heading for the back parking lot and walk quickly in
the opposite direction. On the sidewalk at the edge of campus, I set
my camera on a tripod and look through the lens. I frame my pho-

tograph so that it includes the road and the sidewalk on the other side of the street. I wait. I see a car approach the block, and get ready. It comes whizzing by and I snap the shutter. Soon two more cars come and I photograph them. I stay there all lunch, waiting for cars, taking their pictures as they jet past me. I know this isn't really art. It's only something done out of spite, but each time I press the shutter release I feel better.

22

"This was interesting," Mr. Robertson says. "A real array of songs here." He walks up and down the aisles of desks, dropping our essays facedown. "Only two A's, though. Caitlin, Dylan, nice work. The rest of you didn't go deep enough. There are *layers* of meaning in poetry. You need to look closely, not just skim the surface."

I glance over at Dylan. She sees me and looks away. When Mr. Robertson hands her paper back she drops it into her backpack without even reading what he wrote.

Walking to my locker, I decide on the words to use. It's been a while since I've put any effort into talking to people. When I get there, Dylan glances at me but doesn't say anything. She has a small poster of two girls in her locker.

"Who are they?" I ask.

"They're this band that I like. These cute queer girls from Canada."

"Oh," I say. I think about all the things that I've heard about her and I decide to just ask. It's not like I have anything to lose. "So are you?"

"What." She smirks. "From Canada?"

"No," I say. "Queer." I try to say it as if it isn't the first time I've ever asked someone that, like it's no big thing at all.

She reaches for something in her locker and leans in so far that I can't see her face. I hear her say, "Yeah," and it echoes a little bit.

I try to think of a response, but suddenly my brain is like a television that doesn't work: just static. So I stand there, quiet. She finishes filling up her bag with books and leans toward me.

"This is the part of the conversation," she says, "where *you* tell me something about yourself. Something similar to what I told you. This is where the interrogation turns into an exchange."

"You're asking if *I'm* queer?"

She lifts an eyebrow at me. I feel stupid.

"No," I say. "I'm not."

She closes her locker. "Well, I know it sounds crazy. But I've heard that your kind and my kind can coexist quite peacefully." She smiles and this time it's in a nice way. "I'm going to that noodle place on Webster," she says, and I realize that she isn't going to ask me to come again. She isn't desperate.

"I'll go, too," I say.

We walk out of the science hall.

"Do you have a car?" I ask her.

"*No*," she says, like I just asked if she had a hundred bucks she wanted to loan me. "Do you know how many problems would be solved if people stopped using oil so much? Wars, terrorism, air pollution . . . Just to name a few."

As we step on to the street, Alicia McIntosh stares at us from the window of her boyfriend's Camero. I pretend I don't see her.

23

The noodle place serves Thai soups in huge bowls, but inside it looks like the diner it used to be—posters of Elvis on the wall, lit-up jukebox by the entrance. We slide into opposite sides of a booth with red vinyl seats. Even here, Dylan slouches. She drums her fingers on the table and reads the menu. She doesn't seem to need to talk to be comfortable. I, on the other hand, am desperate for something to say. I read the menu and decide on coconut-milk pineapple soup.

Dylan orders hot and sour soup with mushrooms and green beans and a large coffee. She looks so rowdy, but she's really polite to the waiter. She smiles and says "thanks" like she means it.

"So why did you change your mind?" she asks me.

"What do you mean?"

"I mean what happened the first time? When I asked if you wanted to come. You just weren't hungry or something?"

I'm not used to people being so direct, and I don't know how to answer her. "I can't remember," I say.

She nods slowly, like she knows I'm lying, then looks down at her paper place mat and smiles.

"So what song did you write about?" she asks.

"'Close to Me,'" I say, even though I doubt she's heard it.

"The Cure, right?"

"Yeah, you like them?"

"Sure," she says. "My parents have a couple of their albums."

The waiter brings our drinks to the table.

"Cream and sugar?" he asks her.

"No thanks."

She hunches over her coffee and breathes in the steam.

"So what was your analysis?" she asks.

I open my backpack to get my paper out, and notice that the section holding Ingrid's journal is half unzipped. The top corner of the journal peeks up at me. I yank the zipper closed and pull out my paper, hoping to find a couple sentences that at least sound fairly intelligent.

"'The song deals with feelings of regret,'" I read, "'and not having the ability to know someone well enough, or to understand them completely.'" I stop there and shrug. "Well, there's more," I say. "It goes on."

The waiter brings our soups to the table.

"Thanks so much," Dylan says, looking up at him.

"Thank you," I say after.

We start to fill deep spoons with our soup, holding them for a little while, letting them cool.

"So what did you write about?"

"A Bob Dylan song," she says. "Appropriately." She fishes out a mushroom, then adds, "I'm named after him."

"Oh," I say. "That makes sense."

"I chose 'The Times They Are a-Changin'' but really just used it to talk about how our generation is really different than his, and that it would be great if that song applied to us, but it doesn't. We're complacent."

I'm not really sure what she's talking about, so I just say, "I don't think I know any of his songs."

She doesn't respond, and for a while we just eat. The silence starts getting to me. Not only do I not know a single Bob Dylan song, but I also have nothing interesting to say. She finishes her coffee and asks for another. I look around at the other tables, where people are talking and nodding their heads.

"I heard you got kicked out of your old school for making out with a girl in the bathroom," I blurt.

Her eyebrows rise. She looks into her soup bowl, like it might tell her how to react if she concentrates hard enough. Then she starts to laugh.

"This school is so weird," she says, shaking her head. She brushes a strand of hair away from her face. "I mean, really. And I'm still not over the fact that all the houses in this town are really just one design that was copied over and over and then painted alternating colors." She spoons herself a green bean. "It's no wonder most of the students at Vista are all clones of each other. Before we moved here, I had no idea that a place like this could exist so close to the city."

Even though Los Cerros isn't my favorite place in the world, I feel a little protective of it. "It isn't all like that," I say. "It has some good parts."

"Well, let's go, then," Dylan says. "Show me."

We split the bill, but Dylan leaves the tip because she ends up ordering a third cup of coffee to go.

As we walk out of the restaurant, Dylan says, "By the way, in case you were wondering—my dad got transferred. He can't stand commuting, so we moved."

We head away from the strip mall, past the identical, million-dollar houses, the chain restaurants, the new white, stucco city-hall building with its two skinny, sad palm trees on either side, and onto a narrow gravel street behind it all.

"So, this is it," I say. "My favorite part of Los Cerros." I sweep my arm up to the sky.

It's an old movie theater, standing by itself on a shabby street where no one ever walks or drives. It's hidden, it's out of place, it's run-down and forgotten and empty. But it towers above us, as real as the Starbucks and the Safeway. Most of its windows are boarded up and its paint has mostly peeled off, but someone once painted a mural on the side and you can still see traces of the colors it used to be: yellow and light blue and green. It's falling apart, but I love it.

"The town's going to tear it down," I tell Dylan. The planning has been going on for years, but it's still hard for me to believe that soon it will be gone forever.

Dylan squints against the sun to read the marquee with its missing letters: GO DBYE & THA K YOU.

I can't tell what she sees—a broken-down, rotting old building with weeds waist-high around it, or a place that was clearly amazing before it was forgotten.

Dylan rocks back on her feet, sips her coffee, and heads toward the small circular windows on the four heavy doors. As I watch her peering in, guilt settles in my stomach. The only person I ever came here with was Ingrid. I want to travel back in time a few minutes and decide against leading Dylan here. At the same time I want to join her in her explorations. I want to push my face against the windows like Ingrid and I did a thousand times and stare at the darkened lobby with its empty concession stand.

I wonder if this is what betrayal feels like.

Dylan heads around the side of the theater, but I don't follow her. I know what she'll find: more weeds, a locked back door, a long rectangular window with a heavy curtain on the inside making it impossible to see through.

I sit against the ticket booth to wait for her. Trace my fingers along the edges of the tiled floor. Watch the tips of the weeds sway in the slight breeze. Listen to the traffic sounds from a distant street.

She emerges from the opposite side and leans against the booth.

"I wonder what the last movie that played here was," she says. I smile up at her, feel another pang in my stomach. It's something Ingrid and I used to wonder about all the time.

"I like it here," Dylan says. It sounds simple, honest. "I'm glad I chose you to be friends with."

She pries the plastic lid off her coffee cup and looks disappointedly inside. Empty. I place my hand on my backpack. This is the first afternoon since I discovered it that I haven't gone straight home to read Ingrid's journal.

Without thinking, I say, "We used to sit here all the time."

Facing out, across the street, she says, "Your friend died, didn't she?"

I nod, even though I know she isn't looking at me.

"That's rough," she says, and I'm so used to hearing people tell me things like that, but it's the way that she says it—so calm and solemn—that makes me want to cry.

I don't say anything back for a while. I'm thinking about how Ingrid always made huge elaborate plans for everything. One of them involved getting rich somehow and buying the theater and fixing it up and reopening it to show indie films. Instead of soda, we'd sell tea at the concession stand, and we might even have some photographs or books for sale. It would be more than a theater. It would be a place to escape to when people felt stifled by the chain stores and lonely in their massive houses. I can't understand why she would make plans like that if she wasn't planning on actually doing any of it.

Dylan slides down the side of the ticket booth, until she's sitting next to me. She doesn't try to hug me, she doesn't even sit that close.

I decide that if this is a new friendship, if that's what this is, then I'm going to start things out honestly.

So I say, "It actually feels strange to be here with someone else."

And I don't know how that sounds, and I hope that it doesn't seem like I want her to leave. I hold my breath and she says, "Yeah, it must," and she doesn't sound offended, and she doesn't get up to go, and I am filled with gratitude because it's been way too long since I've just spent time with another person. I'm not ready for it to end yet.

24

It's been weeks since junior year started, and Ms. Delani still isn't looking at me. We spend first period in the dark, looking at projections of famous landscapes. Even though I wish I could hate everything she shows me, I get caught up in the photographs. We start with Ansel Adams, who is pretty overused by now. I mean, his stuff is all over inspirational posters and calendars, but the landscapes are still amazing. The entire front of the classroom goes from waterfalls to forests to mountains to ocean. Looking at them makes me feel small, in a good way.

We move on to Marilyn Bridges. Ms. Delani stands at her desk, stating the obvious.

"Here we have a cityscape. Notice that the sun is brightest on the focal point. The surrounding buildings are in shadow."

She goes through a few more, then says, "Now let me show some examples of student work from past years."

She sits down and opens a new file on her computer. And I know that this is a stupid thing to wish for, but I hope that one of the photos she's about to show will be mine. I know she didn't like my picture of Oakland, but I took so many last year that I thought were pretty good. I took one of the Golden Gate Bridge from right below it, looking up. It was cool because it was of something that's been photographed a million times, but I'd never seen a picture taken from that angle. I picture the image big, covering the wall. In my head I hear Ms. Delani saying, *Excellent work, Caitlin.* I hear it so clearly, every syllable.

An image of cranes on an open field appears on the screen.

"See the nice use of line in this piece?"

Click. Sand and waves and Alcatraz in the distance. *Click.* A strange rock formation. *Click.* A hill with little flowers on it and clear blue sky.

I blink. I've never seen Ingrid's hill this big. The flowers look so full. I can see individual blades of grass. I want to close my eyes and be transported there, to that place, to that day. I remember the ground, cold under my bare feet. Ingrid's purple scarf wrapped around her neck.

Ms. Delani clicks the hill away and there's another landscape, but I don't see it. Instead, I see Ingrid's eyes up close, so blue, the way they looked through the lens of my camera.

Click.

Ingrid's fingers covered in silver rings.

Click.

Her careful, delicate handwriting.

"See how interesting the negative space is here?"

Click.

The huge red sunglasses that covered half her face.

Click.

The pink-and-white scars on her stomach.

"Look at the contrast."

Click.

A deep cut on her arm, bleeding.

Click.

Her eyes, vacant.

Click.

The word *ugly* carved into her hip.

Click.

"The tree in this image is not the focal point. Instead, the shadow is emphasized."

The lights flash on.

Ingrid disappears.

I need to scream, to smash something. I grip the side of my desk so hard that my hand feels like it's about to split open. Ms. Delani stands in front of the room in expensive-looking pin-striped pants and a crisp, button-down shirt. Her hair is smooth and perfect; her skin is perfect; her red glasses frame her eyes perfectly. She walks to the blackboard and starts to write something, but I interrupt her.

"Um . . ." My voice is shaky, loud. I don't know what I want to say, but I know I have to talk. Everything is blurry. "Did you get permission to use those pictures?" I sound crazy, the words come out so loud.

Ms. Delani pauses and lowers the chalk she's holding.

"Which pictures?" she asks.

"All of them," I say. "All of the pictures by students that you showed without even giving them any credit, without even saying their *names*."

No one will look at me. For once, Ms. Delani seems unsure of what to say next. I'm probably spraining my hand, but I can't stop squeezing the desk. Some girls giggle nervously and then Ms.

Delani smiles. She scans the class with bright eyes and says, "Caitlin has made an interesting point. In the future, I will consider asking students for permission to use their work as examples."

Then she pivots toward the board and begins to write.

25

Next period, a freshman comes into class with a yellow slip. My history teacher peers at it.

"Caitlin." He extends his arm, dangling the paper from his fingers like it smells bad. I get up.

"Take your things," he says, and the blood rushes to my face.

I follow the directions on the paper and go to the office. The secretary doesn't look up when I stand at her desk.

"I got this?" I say, and hand her the paper.

She glances at it. "Ms. Haas's office is down the hall," she says.

I trudge down the hall to the office, but the door is closed and I can hear voices inside. My heart starts pounding—did Ms. Delani call my parents? I can picture them in there, sitting next to each other, Mom dabbing her eyes with a tissue, Dad patting her hand and looking worried. The door swings open, and out walks Melanie.

"Oh hey, what's up."

We stand face-to-face in the doorway.

"Nice hair," I blurt, and instantly regret it. For one thing, it isn't true. Mixed in with the brown and blond and orange are now a few strands of blue. I don't think *nice* is what she's going for.

But she ignores me, points her head toward Ms. Haas, and mouths, *Good luck.* Then she slips soundlessly down the hall.

I wait in the doorway for Ms. Haas to notice me. She's pretty old and kind of heavy, but not in a bad way. Her gray hair is pulled back in a bun and she's wearing purple feathers as earrings.

She sees me and says, "You must be Caitlin. Come in."

Ms. Haas is the school therapist. Although I have been invited many times, this is the first time I've been in her office. It's small and decorated in a way that's a little too inviting. The floor is covered with a bright yellow shag rug, and all the chairs are big and soft. Trees and sunsets and other nonthreatening images hang on the walls. I swear one of the pictures is by Ansel Adams—below a tall, strong-looking tree, the caption reads: *Sky's the limit*. Disgusting. I choose the chair farthest away from Ms. Haas's desk and try not to sink too far into it.

She introduces herself and talks about all the "wonderful services" she's here to provide. I try to tune her out. When she's finished, she asks me, "Do you know why you're here?"

"Yeah," I say.

She beams. "Great. Why?"

"Because Ms. Delani doesn't know how to deal with anything or even communicate *at all*, so she feels the need to hand me over to you," I say.

Ms. Haas leans back in her chair and clasps her hands together. I move my shoe across the shag rug, make the yellow darker, then lighter, then darker again. I wait for Ms. Haas to respond.

Then, finally, she says, "I hear that you and Ingrid Bauer were close friends."

My stomach clenches up. I stop moving my foot and shrug.

"Maybe you would like to spend some time talking with me about her."

She waits, and when I don't say anything she says, "Maybe you would like to tell me how you felt when you were with her? What was special about your friendship?"

I try to sit up a little more in the chair, but it's too soft. I say, "I don't understand your question. I don't know what you want me to tell you."

"Okay," she says, her voice full of patience. "I'll tell you where I'm going with this. I'd like to help you voice any feelings of guilt or anger or depression that you might be feeling and to work with you to overcome those feelings. Now"—she leans toward me— "tell me what *you* would like."

I look up from the rug to her face. She's smiling in the nicest way.

"What I would like," I say, "is to go back to class."

26

I leave school directly from the office and walk to my house the back way so no one will catch me. When I get home, I shut the door to my room even though no one else is there, just because it feels good to be alone, surrounded by my tacked-up band posters and magazine clippings. I unzip Ingrid's journal from its pocket and sit down on the chair in the corner by the window. I open to the next entry, hoping Ingrid won't be drooling all over Ms. Delani again.

DEAR JAYSON,

tonight i was outside late with caitlin and we were just
laying on the grass in her backyard looking up at the sky
and all i wanted was to talk about you but i could tell
she was getting annoyed. i don't know why, it's not like
she had something totally compelling to discuss with me
or anything. sometimes i feel like i can't wait for her to
find someone to crush on so that i don't have to feel
so bad when all i want to talk about is your arms your
hands your face your neck your voice your mouth. your
mouth. i can barely sit next to you anymore in bio. i can
feel my skin burning up when you're that close. my life is
just waiting for you to get started. i want you to touch
me. i want you to take my clothes off. when it happens
i want it to hurt so hard it snaps me back in place. it
would last for ages and when it ended i would be a whole
person again. not sick. not crazy. it would be something
permanent. jayson, if i let you see what's in my head
would you think i was crazy? everything gets so messed-
up and twisted. every time i try to do something right
it backfires. would you freak out? would you understand?
would you tell everyone in school that i was weird and
sick? whenever i see your arms i want them around me and
i know that sounds cheesy but nothing has ever felt as
good as that would feel.

love,
ingrid

I propel myself out of the chair and into my closet, holding Ingrid's journal gingerly, like it's too hot to touch. I pull all my clothes out of my hamper, drop the journal to the bottom, and stuff the clothes back on top.

It wasn't unfair to not want to talk about Jayson every single minute. I mean, I always went along with plans she made to try to bump into him and to casually walk by his house after school sometimes, hoping he'd see us. Just because I wanted to talk about something different for a few minutes a day doesn't mean that she had to write that about me. And that whole hurting thing? Ingrid and I felt the same about almost everything, so I don't really understand. Maybe I misunderstood it. Whatever, it doesn't matter. I don't want to think about it anymore.

I go outside. I walk past my parents' garden, where their parsnips are beginning to sprout, to the heap of wood. I pull a long plank off the pile and start to drag it away, down the slope of our backyard. It's heavier than I thought it would be. I pull the plank past the brick patio, past the flowers, up and over this little hill, to the part where the land stops looking like a backyard and more just like a grassy area with a bunch of trees, almost dense enough to be a forest. I drop the wood at the base of the tree I like best. It's a big oak. I used to climb it when I was a kid. After I catch my breath, I start back toward the house to get more. If I ever figure out something to build, I'm not going to do it with everyone watching.

Later, my parents call me down to the kitchen. I find Mom washing lettuce and Dad heating olive oil and garlic in a pan.

"What?" I ask them.

Dad turns to me. "Well, hello to you, too," he says.

He's taken his tie off and unbuttoned the first two buttons of his dress shirt. He holds his arm out to hug me, but I pretend I don't notice and open the freezer instead. The cold feels good.

"How was your day, sweetheart?" my mom asks.

"Okay. Do you want help?"

"You could chop that onion," she says.

I grab a knife from the drawer.

My dad continues some story he must have started to tell my mom before I came down. At first I try to listen, but I have no idea who he's talking about. I cut the onion in half and my eyes burn.

A minute later, the phone rings and my dad hits the speaker button.

"Hello?"

We wait. A recorded voice comes on.

"This is the Vista High School office of attendance calling to report that your child missed one or more periods today. The absence will be marked as unexcused unless we receive a doctor's note or notification from a parent or guardian explaining that the absence was due to a family emergency."

My dad stops stirring. My mom turns the water off. I stand with my back to the phone, chopping.

Shit. I forgot about the phone calls.

"Caitlin, did you cut school?" Mom's voice is straining to be patient.

I stop chopping and turn around, thinking maybe they'll feel bad when they see what their onion is doing to my eyes. But they just stare at me.

I can't think of a good excuse, so I just tell them, "I hate my photo teacher."

"Ms. Delani?" Mom's eyebrows lift in surprise.

"You liked her last year," Dad says. My parents glance at each other, but they don't say anything. I can see my mom get frustrated. Her lips are tight and she starts taking all these short breaths. Dad sighs.

Finally, he says, "Caitlin, you can't ditch school. There are going

to be a lot of people in your life who you won't like and you're going to have to learn to deal with them."

"Ms. Delani is a very, *very* nice woman," my mom says. "She
taught you and Ingrid so much last year."

"She didn't teach me anything," I say. "I wish I'd never met her."

I turn to look out the window but it's dark, so all I see is us,
reflected. The most unlikely of family portraits. My mother, an
apron tied over her suit, her hair falling out of a barrette; my father, leaning against the oven, one hand rubbing his forehead in
exasperation; and me, staring straight at the lens, onion tears drying on my face. I try to think of some way to explain this situation
to them, but my mom is going on and on about the dangers and
consequences of skipping school until it seems so absurd that she's
reacting like this over something so small.

"Why are you laughing?" Mom asks me, her voice hurt and
angry.

"I can't help it," I say, giggling now. "You're acting psychotic."

She stops talking. She stares at me hard, then wipes her hands
on her apron. Calmly, she walks to the stove and turns it off. She
turns toward me and I brace myself for a hug. But she brushes
past me, lifts the cutting board from the counter, and scrapes the
chopped onion in the trash can.

"I'll be in our room," she says to my dad, and leaves the kitchen.

27

I eat three grape Popsicles for dinner and keep a few Cure songs
playing over and over pretty loud so I won't drive myself crazy trying to hear if my parents are talking about me. I don't care about
not getting along with them. I mean, it's completely normal, right?
I can't think of anyone who always gets along with her parents.
Ingrid used to fight with Susan and Mitch all the time, even though
I thought they were pretty nice. Still, I keep waiting for a knock on

my bedroom door because we're just not like that, my parents and me. We snap at one another sometimes but we don't really fight.

The knock comes about an hour later, just a light tapping on the door that I can't hear over the music at first.

"Honey?" Mom says. "Someone's here to see you." I can tell from her voice that she's just talking to me out of obligation. She hasn't forgiven me yet.

I walk to my door and open it. My mom's eyes are swollen and her mascara is smeared off. It hurts to look at her.

"Should I send him up?" she asks.

"Okay." I peer skeptically at my sweatpants and ratty T-shirt; whoever it is, he is not going to see me at my best.

Mom patters back downstairs.

I hear her say, "Go on up. Last door on the left."

Quickly, I throw the covers over my bed, trying to fake some semblance of order.

"Hey," says a guy's voice.

I turn around.

Taylor Riley is standing in my room.

"What are you doing here?"

"Oh," he says, looking confused. "Well, we're having a quiz tomorrow in precalc. He just announced it today. And it's on the homework but you don't know what the homework is, so I thought I should come tell you. You know, in case you wanted to, like, glance over it or something."

I don't answer him because I'm staring at his shirt. It says, in big letters across the front, WILL WORK FOR SEX.

He looks at me. "What's wrong? Is there something on my . . ."

He looks down at himself. I watch his face turn pink and then red.

"Oh my God," he says. "Oh shit. I completely forgot I was wearing this. Oh my God, your mom. I can't believe she let me into your room."

He looks so embarrassed, and I would laugh except for how weirded out I am that he came over to my house to tell me about the homework.

"Do you think she noticed?" he asks.

"It's kind of hard not to."

"Yeah, but does she wear glasses usually? I mean, she wasn't. So maybe she couldn't really read it because it was blurry?"

I say, "She doesn't wear glasses," and I can't help but laugh because he's acting so funny and his face looks red next to his blond hair and those sideburns. "So what *is* the homework?"

"Pages eighty-seven to eighty-nine. Odd problems only," he recites.

"Thanks."

"Okay," he says. "Well, you can study now."

Then he pulls his shirt up over his head. I look at my feet.

"What are you doing?"

"Turning my shirt inside out. Just in case I run into your dad on my way downstairs."

"Why do you have that shirt anyway?"

He shrugs. "Jayson and I saw it in Berkeley at one of those T-shirt stores and I thought it was funny. I guess it's kind of lame."

I don't want to think about Ingrid's journal entry again, so instead I think about what I would do if Taylor started to kiss me. I imagine him reaching out for me. I would forget about everything bad for a little while.

My face gets hot. The real Taylor is right here, standing in front of me, apparently at a loss for words. Now his shirt says XES ROF KROW LLIW.

"Thanks for giving me the assignment. I mean, it was kind of weird for you to just show up here. But, thanks."

"No worries," he says. He turns and walks to my door and stops. Then he says, "That thing you told me about Ingrid? I guess that was your way of telling me that it was jacked up of me to ask how she did it. So I guess I also came to tell you that I'm sorry if it seemed like that to you. I didn't mean anything by it." He stops and I can see that he's thinking about something. Finally, he says, "It was harsh, though, the way you told me. I learned the stages of grief once. I think you might be in the anger stage."

He says it from across the room, but it feels like he just reached out, grabbed me by the throat, and squeezed me there. I feel my eyes well up. I can't think of anything to say to him, so I just look at the carpet and he says, "See you," and then I'm alone in my room again.

I retrieve Ingrid's journal, ready to break my one-entry-a-day rule. But then I put it down. I need something that will listen and talk back. I rifle through my drawer for the school directory and open it to *Schuster*. There's Dylan's number next to a pixelated photo of her glowering for the camera.

I recognize her voice when she answers. It isn't low but it's kind of raspy.

"Hi," I say. "This is Caitlin."

"Oh, hey," she says, and I'm so thankful at the way she says it, like it's totally normal for me to call her.

"So, um. I have to do this photo assignment tomorrow after school? And I was wondering if you might want to come with me. We could go to the noodle place or somewhere before."

"Yeah, sounds good," Dylan says. I hear her mumble something in the background. "So I'll meet you at our lockers?"

"Okay, cool," I say, and I'm glad she isn't here to see me nodding my head up and down over and over like an idiot.

I hang up and go outside again, but this time I climb into my car. I turn the tape on and listen until I fall asleep.

28

I thought it would be easy to find a bad landscape, but it isn't. Even things that are ugly and plain in real life look different once I'm looking through the camera. Everything small turns significant. The gaps between branches on a sad little shrub transform into a striking example of negative space. I pivot around to face the strip mall. I half expect some miracle, but it remains ugly through the lens. I'm about to snap a picture when Dylan stops me.

"Wait," she says. "Your teacher's going to think that you're making a statement. She's going to be like, 'Caitlin, fabulous commentary on our consumerist culture,' or something."

I lower the camera. "You're right. We need to find a place that's all just dirt."

Dylan sips her coffee, says, "There's this place that's like a block from my house where the land's all leveled."

We start walking.

Dylan lives in the opposite direction from me, on the newer side of town. The houses there are mostly huge. Some of them are trying to look Spanish with white stucco exteriors and clay tile roofs. Others are just gigantic, modern boxes.

We get there and stop. "This is exactly what I wanted," I say, staring at a dirt lot.

"I think someone's going to build a house here."

I start messing with the aperture on my camera.

"What are you doing?"

"I want it to be overexposed and out of focus."

Dylan laughs. "So why, exactly, do you want your picture to suck so badly?"

"The photo teacher hates me and I hate her."

"Sounds healthy."

Dylan watches me take a couple of pictures of the dirt. The light outside is just the way I want it—not too bright. The contrast of the dirt against the sky will be almost nonexistent. After I've snapped a couple shots, Dylan shakes her head.

"*Why* does she hate you?"

I try to think of a way to explain it that won't make her freak out the way my parents did. I stop messing with the camera and sit down on the curb next to her.

"It's hard to explain. I was in her class last year, with Ingrid. She was actually nice then. But Ingrid's like this amazing photographer." I stop. "Or she *was*, I mean. An amazing photographer. So Ms. Delani was really nice to me because I was always with Ingrid."

"And she isn't nice anymore?"

"She just completely ignores me."

Dylan nods. She watches me closely. "Okay," she finally says. "So you're doing this to get her attention."

"No," I say, and it comes out a little harsher than I meant it to. "It's just that I don't see the point in trying to put effort into her class."

Dylan leans back on the sidewalk and stares up at the sky. I untie my shoes and then tie them again, tighter.

"I don't want to sound like an asshole or anything," she says after a while, "but it seems like there's more going on. We just walked half a mile so that you could take a picture of dirt. So it seems like you *are* putting effort into this. You really want to piss her off."

"Oh," I say. "So you're an all-around genius? You don't have to save it up for English papers?"

She laughs. "I'm thirsty, are you thirsty?"

We walk up one more block to Dylan's house, which is smaller than the others, painted dark blue.

"You have an old house."

"Yeah, my parents aren't into these monstrosities," she says, gesturing to the three-story beige houses that tower above her little one.

"Look," she says. "We actually have a white picket fence. I told my parents that if they were going to move me to the suburbs, they'd better go all out. Watch: isn't this fantastic?"

She stops on the sidewalk and then skips through the fence. And it *is* funny, Dylan in her dark, tough clothes, her messy hair, and smudged eye makeup, entering a white picket fence.

Dylan's living room is decorated with all of these old prints that look kind of scientific. They each have one type of flower or fruit printed on them with the plant's name in small letters across the bottom. When we get to her room, I look at the stuff on her desk as she puts her backpack down and takes off her sweater. She has a laptop and pad of paper and a mug with a bunch of pens in it. Next to it, there's a photo in a thin, silver frame of a girl with short, light hair and a wide smile.

"Who's this?" I ask her.

"That's Maddy," she says.

"Does she go to your old school?"

"Yeah." Dylan opens a window by her bed. "We've been together for five months."

"Wow," I say. I start my crazy nodding. I can't seem to stop or to think of anything else to say. I want her to know that I'm not weirded out or anything, so I say, "That's really cool!" It comes out way too enthusiastically and Dylan raises an eyebrow at me.

I look at a bulletin board above her desk and see a picture of an adorable little boy. He's wearing rain boots and playing in the sand. The photo has this old snapshot quality that I really wish I could pull off. It's softly focused and the colors are muted in a way that makes me feel nostalgic just looking at it.

"I love this picture."

Dylan looks at it, then looks away.

"Okay. Something to drink," she says. "Follow me."

We walk down the hall and into a kitchen with bright yellow walls and a million pots and pans hanging from a metal rack over the stove.

"Mom's a cook. Like, as her job. She's really into her kitchen. When we were looking for houses, my dad would go straight to the backyards, I would head back to check out the bedrooms, and my mom would go directly into the kitchens. This was the first house we all agreed on. So we took it."

She grabs two glasses from a cabinet.

"Water? Juice? Soda?"

"Water's good."

"Plain or fizzy."

"Fizzy."

"So," Dylan says, handing me a glass. "Do you want to go to the city with me tomorrow? I'm meeting Maddy and some of our friends."

"Sure," I say, and take a sip so she won't see me smiling.

When I get home, I drop the camera off in my room and head back downstairs. I unlock the door to my car and climb into the backseat, but for some reason I can't get comfortable. It feels kind of cramped or dark back there. I haul my backpack up to the front, and squeeze my way into the passenger seat. The view is different from up here—I can see more of the house, the patio. Actually, I can see more of everything.

I take Ingrid's journal out of my backpack, prop my knees on the dashboard, and read.

DEAR PINK PEELING PAINT,

you are an example of whatdoyoucallit? alliteration! but
you're also pretty and sad the way i'm pretty and sad,
getting sadder and sadder all the time as the pretty layer
comes off in strips. that is a metaphor or something.
caitlin would know what to call it and she would probably
say something like 'snap out of it' or 'what's up with
you this morning' or something kind of harsh like that. she
doesn't know what it feels like to feel like me. earlier i
was shaving my legs and i pressed the razor down hard
at this certain angle and it cut pretty deep but not deep
enough. i always get this feeling like if i could just get
a little deeper i could get through the day. i would feel
so much better. but it just doesn't work. i'm gonna have
to find a real blade the kind in movies that the tough men
use in dirty low-lit bathrooms while they look in the dirty
mirror and mutter to themselves. but even with the regular
razor blood seeped through the knee socks i wanted to
wear today. i discovered it near my ankle already getting
brown before i left the house so i had to take them off
and stuff them in the trash and put on some pants and run
to meet caitlin who is starting to get worried or suspect
me or something. her face gets all serious and she stares
at me when she thinks i don't notice her doing it. i'm trying
to be good and take all the pills my mom keeps giving me
but they make me zone out and i can't think clearly. jayson
isn't in bio today. basically, everything is a total waste. i
am a total waste.

LOVE,
INGRID

I finish reading and shove the journal into the glove compartment. I wish I knew why she never told me any of this. Maybe she thought I wouldn't be able to handle it, that I was too sheltered or too innocent or something. If she had told me why she cut herself all the time, or that it was the pills that made her act so spaced out, or that she was even on pills, or even saw doctors, or *any* of it, I would have done my best to help her. I'm not saying I'm a superhero. I'm not saying I would have just swooped down and saved her. I'm just saying the only reason everything was a waste was that she made it a waste. That whole time, back when I was just a normal kid in high school, living out my normal life, I really thought everything mattered.

29

The next day in precalc, Taylor strides past his usual seat and takes the desk in front of me. He doesn't say hi or anything. He just sits there with his back to me like it's normal. Mr. James hands our quizzes back to us. I got an 89 percent. I scribble on my paper, trying to figure out the problems I missed.

Taylor turns around and stares down at my quiz.

"Hey, look," he says. He shows me his. "We got the exact same grade. Crazy."

"Yeah," I say, kind of sarcastically, but I'm glad that he's sitting here, talking to me.

"If anyone has any questions about the quiz, you can see me after class," Mr. James says. "We'll go over the homework in a few minutes, but first I want to introduce a new project. This will be a little different. I want you to find a partner and choose a mathematician from anywhere in the world—past or present—and prepare a presentation for the class that discusses the mathematician's life, achievements, and historical and political setting." He keeps talking about how math doesn't only happen in classrooms, how it's connected to everyday life. Taylor turns to face me again.

"Wanna work together?" he asks.

"Sure," I whisper, and feel blood pump in my ears.

He turns back.

Mr. James says, "When you've broken into pairs, let me know."

Taylor's hand shoots into the air.

"Yes?"

"Me and Caitlin'll work together," he says, and then hunches over, suddenly fascinated by his quiz. I can feel the eyes of all the other students staring at us. My face feels hot.

But Mr. James, unaware that guys like Taylor are only supposed to want to work with the Alicia McIntoshes of the school, just mumbles, "Taylor and Caitlin," and writes our names down, together, on a sheet of paper.

30

When I get to the library, Dylan is talking to the study-hall teacher, so I stay out of their way and look through a stack of art books.

I glance over at Dylan but she's still talking. She sees me and mouths, *Just a second.*

I start picking books off a stack. There's one about Brazilian music and one about bridges and one about decorating small spaces.

Then I find one with a photo of a treehouse on the cover. I open it up, expecting to see all these simple treehouses built for little kids, but that's not what the book's about at all. These are real houses. People actually live in them, and they're built up on high branches and they look amazing. They are tiny and private and warm. A bunch of them have built-in bookshelves and desks. I had no idea that treehouses like these existed.

Suddenly Dylan's behind me.

"Hey," she says. "Sorry. Ready to go?"

I don't even look at her. I can't stop looking through the pages of the book. Not only are there photographs, but there are lists of supplies you need to build your own, illustrated step-by-step directions.

All I can think about are the stacks and stacks of wood planks just waiting for me to put them to use.

"Let's go, come on," Dylan says.

"Okay," I say. "Yeah. I just have to check this out first."

31

When we walk up the escalator from underground at the Sixteenth and Mission BART station, there are panhandlers everywhere, asking us for money, food, cigarettes, to buy the papers they're selling, to give them change for a BART ticket so they can get home. I feel caught in a stampede, but Dylan just handles them.

"Sorry, man," she says to a boy who looks just a few years older than us, holding an angry dog on a leash.

To the ruder men who get up in our way as we're walking, she says simple, hard no's.

Whenever Ingrid and I got out of the suburbs, into Berkeley or San Francisco, and saw how other people lived, Ingrid would cry at the smallest things—a little boy walking home by himself, a stray cat with loose skin and fur draped over bones, a discarded cardboard sign saying HUNGRY PLEASE HELP. She would snap a picture, and by the time she lowered her camera, the tears would already be falling. I always felt kind of guilty that I didn't feel as sad as she did, but now, watching Dylan, I think that's probably a good thing. I mean, you see a million terrible things every day, on the news and in the paper, and in real life. I'm not saying that it's stupid to feel sad, just that it would be impossible to let everything get to you and still get some sleep at night.

I walk fast with Dylan up Eighteenth to Valencia and then across to Guererro, until we finally reach Dolores Street and I see the park.

"This is my old school." Dylan points to an old, grand building across from the public tennis courts and a bus shelter. "And those," she says, pointing to a group of kids sitting under a tree, "are my friends."

We walk toward them, and as we get closer, they come into focus: a boy with delicate arms wearing dark jeans that actually fit him, a couple—a boy and a girl—their backs against a tree trunk, their fingers clasped together.

"Dylan!" they all call out, their voices rising over one another's.

I smile nervously. I can just tell from the way they're sitting, so comfortably, that they're so much cooler than I'll ever be. They look different from the people at my school. My mom would say they look worldly.

Dylan and I sit down on the grass with them and I listen to them all talk. I don't say anything but it's not because they aren't including me. It's just nice to sit back and listen. Half of the conversation is directed to me. They tell me all these stories about themselves and one another. There is one about an all-night diner on Church Street, and how the boy in the jeans had a crush on a waitress who worked the night shift. He snuck out of his house every night and stayed for hours while she refilled his coffee.

"Oh!" he says, his face all lit up with excitement. "And here's the best part: her name was Vicky. She wore this little apron over her skirt. It was so retro."

"So what happened?" I ask. "Did you ever talk to her?"

"No," he says, sighing. "She just stopped working. One night I went and she wasn't there. And then she never came back again."

"It was a tragedy," Dylan says. "He's never gotten over it." She smirks at him and he swats her leg with his sweater.

They start another story. This one is about the couple, who have been together for almost a year, and the way the girl followed the guy for two quarters before finally having the courage to introduce herself. I lie on the grass with my head propped on my backpack and watch all the people walking by us on the grass. I imagine what it would be like to go to a school so big that people don't know one another.

After a while it's time to go meet Maddy at her job. We all stand up and walk to the edge of the park. They hug one another as I stand aside, and then they wave to me and we break off into three directions.

It's just Dylan and me again. She rocks backward and then forward on her feet, puts her hands through her messy hair, and says, "We need coffee, right?"

Inside the café, Dylan pulls a silver cigarette holder from her back pocket. She snaps it open and I see a few rolled-up bills between its mirrored sides. She pays for her coffee and I buy a cookie, turn, and see her at a table peering into the cigarette case. She squints her eyes, opens them wide, and smears some black stuff around them. Then she snaps the case shut and starts tapping nervously against the table.

"Are you okay?" I ask her.

"Me? Yeah. Let's walk." She's up and out the door in seconds and I'm dodging bicyclists and strollers trying to keep up.

We walk for a million sunny blocks, past palm trees and cafés and Laundromats, until we reach a small store on a corner. It's red-and-white-striped, like an oversize, square candy cane with the words COPY CAT painted on the front. We stop outside and Dylan looks at her reflection in the window. She moves a strand of hair away from her face and then moves it back. She turns around and announces, in a louder voice than usual, "Maddy's shift should be over in two minutes." She says this like I am part of a walking tour and Maddy is the most important of landmarks.

I start to think of how I could tease her about this, when the glass door opens and a girl with light, wavy hair walks out of the store. She has big dark eyes, and when she sees us a smile blooms across her face. And as Dylan turns to look at her, I watch this amazing thing happen. Dylan, in her skintight black jeans, safety-pinned shirt, and bulky armbands, with her hair sticking out in every direction and that black freshly smeared around her eyes, doesn't just smile, doesn't just walk toward Maddy and put her arms around her. No. Instead, every muscle in her whole body seems to lose all tension, her step forward resembles a skip, and she lets out a *hey* that might as well say, *I love you, you are so beautiful, no one in the world is as amazing as you are.*

32

Sitting at an outdoor table at a café a few blocks from Copy Cat, Maddy leans over the round, green tabletop and says, "Caitlin, tell me about yourself. What do you enjoy doing?"

It's the kind of question I'd expect parents to ask a guy you wanted to date. It sounds so adult, but for some reason I kind of like it. She cocks her head and waits for an answer. Dylan is leaning back in her metal chair, rubbing her finger against the snaps of her leather bracelet.

Maddy looks at me as intently as Dylan does, but in a different way. When Dylan stares at me it's like she's looking through me, learning all the things about me that I don't even know. Maddy just looks focused. It makes me think for a second. I want to say photography, but it's only been a day since Dylan watched as I took the worst photograph imaginable. How would I look if I admitted that I was purposely failing at something I loved?

So I say, "I like building things." I listen to the words as they come out, testing how they make me sound.

Maddy looks interested and Dylan glances up from her bracelet.

"Out of wood," I add.

"So you're an artist," Maddy says. "That's fantastic. What do you build?"

I try to figure out how to tell the truth without making myself sound really lame. I decide to focus on the future. "I'm about to build a treehouse," I say. "But not like a kid one."

"Like the ones in that book you just checked out?" Dylan asks. She sips her coffee—her third refill of the afternoon.

"Yeah," I say. "I have this great tree in my backyard I'm going to use."

Maddy looks excited. "My parents have a friend in Oregon who has a treehouse on his property. It's so beautiful. I sit up there all the time when we visit him. I'd love to see yours when you finish it."

"Yeah," I say. "Definitely, you should."

"Maddy's an actor," Dylan tells me, resting her hand on Maddy's back.

"That's so cool," I say. "I took drama one semester but I wasn't that good. I got stage fright."

Maddy says, "I used to get nervous before performances, too, but it went away. Now I have a ritual that I do before the production starts where I imagine a light around me, protecting me from what everyone in the audience thinks. It sounds strange, but it works."

She explains this so confidently that I'm convinced. I ask, "So are you going to move to L.A. after you graduate?"

"Oh, no," Maddy says. She shakes her head, and her white shell earrings sway back and forth. "I'm only interested in theater."

I sip the macchiato I ordered and wish I'd gotten something different. I like the little cups they come in, and all the foam, but the actual drink is so bitter. I haven't discovered the right coffee drink yet.

"So, Dylan," I say. "What do *you* enjoy?"

Dylan shrugs. "I'm still finding myself," she says.

Maddy laughs. "She just doesn't like to brag. She's crazy smart. Do you know how she spent five straight summers of her life?"

Dylan laughs. "Shut up," she says to Maddy, but she says it sweetly.

"Physics camp!" Maddy shouts. Then she repeats it, solemnly: "*Physics* camp."

It's hard to believe. All the science geeks at school spend their lunch period in little clusters, talking about acceptance rates at MIT. And rarely is anyone good at both science and English.

Dylan shrugs. "We got to make electromagnets and measure light and stuff. It was fun."

We sit for a while longer, just talking, and I wonder what it would be like to be really passionate about something. I thought photography was it for me. I thought I loved it and I was good at it. Now it turns out that I only loved it.

"I'll be right back," Dylan says. She gets up from the table and Maddy smiles at her retreating figure, all long skinny limbs and shoulder blades and wild hair.

When Dylan's back inside the café, Maddy says, "I'm glad she found you. She was worried that she wouldn't find any friends in Los Cerros."

I fidget in my seat. "Yeah," I say. "It's a pretty small school."

"I'm sorry to hear about your friend."

I stare, startled, into my macchiato cup. It's still full and getting colder.

"I'm sorry," Maddy says. "I know it must seem strange for me to say that. But I wanted to let you know that Dylan lost someone, too. It's not something she likes to talk about, so please don't mention anything. But know that she understands what you're going through. She's an amazing person. I'm also glad that *you* found *her*."

33

On the way home from the city, I sit next to Maddy in the back-seat of Dylan's mom's car and wonder how it works when Maddy spends the night. I mean, her mom obviously knows that they're a couple. Do they both sleep in Dylan's room?

Dylan twists around in her seat as we pull up to my house. "So, want to hang out at lunch on Monday?" she asks me.

"Yeah," I say. "Meet me at our lockers?"

"Great," Dylan says.

I thank her mom for the ride and I'm about to tell Maddy that it was nice to meet her when she unbuckles her seat belt and leans over to hug me. "It was so nice to meet you," she says. "I really hope we can see each other again soon."

I hug her back. When we let go, Dylan and her mom are both looking at us, smiling. I want to spend the rest of my life in this car. I want to be frozen in time here, prop my knees up on the back of Dylan's seat, and just stay. But the lights glow through the curtains of my house, and I open my car door to the night.

"Bye," I say.

Together, they say good-bye back.

Inside, my parents ask how my day was.

"Good," I say, beaming. "It was really good."

They search my face for sarcasm. When they don't find it, they exchange curious, smiling looks.

As I'm brushing my teeth, I think of Dylan and me, walking in the city with the buildings high all around us. Even the air there seems more awake. I decide that we should go there every day, a few times a week at least. As I turn off my light and burrow under the covers, I imagine myself in the future, lounging under a tree with Dylan's friends who are now my friends. I look like them, I'm wearing clothes that look great on me. We're telling stories to someone new.

A minute later, I switch the light back on.

Ingrid.

I get her journal out and read.

DEAR CAITLIN,

when you left my house today i started crying and couldn't stop. there are so many things that i want so badly to tell you but i just can't. sometimes i think my mom's the crazy one. she makes the biggest deal out of these tiny microscopic things that aren't that weird. but when i can tell that you aren't understanding me that's when i know that i've really lost it. you look at me and i can see something in your face, it's like you don't know who i am for a second and it throws me. i get paralyzed. then i wonder about everything i do. like, is it normal that i just put five spoons of sugar in my tea and is it normal that i switched on the light to my room before i walked in instead of just walking in and switching it on after and is it normal that sometimes i look in the mirror and think i'm fucking gorgeous and sometimes i look and i think i'm a disgusting slob? i've been doing all this reading online every night. there are normal people who go crazy and think they're hitler and spend every minute sobbing 'i'm sorry i'm sorry'. and there are people who are too scared to ever leave the house, or even their rooms so they spend the rest of their lives there alone. and there are people who kill their children because they're convinced god told them to and i am so scared all the time that i'm going to turn into that. every day i want to tell you about all the pills i have to take and how the doctors are constantly evaluating my every move and writing in their little notebooks and all i want to do is read what they write about me. what the fuck are they writing about me? and i want to tell you about everything but i can't because i couldn't stand for you to have that look on your face all the time. i just need you to look at me and think that i'm normal. i just really need that from you.

LOVE,
INGRID

My chest is caving in on itself. I never thought I was perfect, I never even thought I was close, but I never knew how terrible I actually was. Now that I do know, regret fills me. Like the times that we would change in the locker room, and Ingrid would stare at herself in the mirror and say, *How can you stand to look at me? I am so gross.* I wouldn't even look at her. I hardly heard it. I thought she was just being annoying, or looking for compliments like everyone else. I didn't know how scared she was and I should have, because that's what friends do: they notice things. They're there for each other. They see what parents don't. If I could do it again, I would stand with her in front of the locker-room mirror and tell her about all the amazing things I saw in her. And all the times when she got all freaked out and quiet, I shouldn't have left. Instead, I should have put some music on the stereo and sat back against the wall on one side of her room, and hoped that even if I couldn't get into the dark places in her head, I would at least be there waiting on the outside. And maybe most of all I shouldn't have turned away from all of the cuts and burns and bruises she gave herself. I should have noticed all of them because they were a part of her. She deserved for someone to see her as clearly as they could. To make that effort to understand.

My best friend is dead, and I could have saved her. It's so wrong, so completely and painfully wrong, that I walked through my front door tonight smiling.

winter

1

I walk to school as dawn breaks. I'm awake and alert, numb and exhausted. I never knew I could be all these things at the same time, but here I am, headed to school, eyelids heavy, breathing in the cold air.

An hour and a half before school starts the campus is a ghost town—no cars in the parking lot, no buses in the front circle, no people anywhere.

I break into the photo lab.

Ingrid and I used to do this all the time. There's only one window. It's along the back of the building where the shrubs are overgrown, and nobody ever goes. I guess the custodian just doesn't know about it. Once, Ingrid and I unlocked it from the inside, and as far as I know, it hasn't been locked since.

I pry it open and drop my backpack over, hoist myself up, and climb into the room. I shut the window and, for a minute, I just stand in the complete darkness. Then I feel my way to the darkroom.

Maybe it's because I hardly slept last night, maybe the darkness is putting me in a dream state, but as I shut the darkroom
door behind me, I can see Ingrid clearly. She flips on a safety light
and stands in the red glow, takes a roll of film from her bag. In
her yellow dress, with bare feet, she is the only thing illuminated,
surrounded by blackness. Her back is to me. Each time she turns,
I can see her profile. I want to touch her, but I stay on my side
of the room. If I stay completely still, this moment might last
forever.

Without turning, she says, *I shot an amazing roll yesterday.*

Of what?

*I was just sitting in my room and this little bird landed on a branch
by my window.*

Just sitting? What were you thinking about?

*Oh, I don't know. Nothing. The little thing stayed there for me,
hopped from branch to branch as I took picture after picture.*

I found your journal. You meant for me to find it, right?

*Then, when he started to fly away he lifted up, and flapped his
wings so fast that they were just two blurs on either side of him.*

I didn't know you were scared.

*It was like he was waiting for me, like he knew it would make a
great picture. I got at least three shots of him hovering in the air like
that before he flew away.* She finally turns to me. Her clear blue eyes,
her crooked smile. She brushes a blond curl away from her face with
her wrist, careful not to get the photo chemicals on her cheek. A
sharp pain shoots up my chest. I've forgotten to breathe. *Of course
you knew I was scared. There was just nothing you could do.*

It hurts to look. I shut my eyes. When I open them, the room is
quiet and empty. She is gone again.

I guide myself to the counter, pop open my film canister. The
long negative strip tumbles into my open hands. I grope for the
reel and slide in the film, fill the plastic canister with developing
chemicals.

I barely have time to process this and wait for the negatives to dry. My landscape is due at eight o'clock.

2

All through fourth period the popular girls in the back corner write urgent notes to one another, the teacher sits over our quizzes with a red pen in his hand, a man's deep voice wavers from the television speakers about the vastness of the universe, and I feel something poisonous in the pit of my stomach. If I could think of any way to make it sound rational, I'd meet Dylan at our lockers like I said I would and explain what I realized last night: it's a huge responsibility to be a friend, and I just can't handle it right now.

But when the bell rings, I grab my notebook and stick it in my backpack and try to make it out the door before anyone else. I think about hiding in a bathroom, but I'm too nervous to stay in one place, so I keep going until I reach the back parking lot, headed toward the bus stop. I'll just ride the bus all the way through one route, till it takes me back here, and by then lunch will be over. Before I make it through the parking lot, though, I spot the hall monitor patrolling the edge of campus, bullhorn in hand. He sees me, lifts the bullhorn to his mouth. I make a sharp left and walk fast toward the baseball field. And that's when I remember Melanie.

She's sitting with some other kids on the bleachers, just like she told me. Usually, I wouldn't even consider approaching a group of kids I hardly know. It takes a certain kind of person to do that. But this is a moment of desperation, and they're already looking at me through the fence. It would seem strange if I turned around now. I step through a hole in the fence where the chains have been cut; my backpack snares on a wire. I have to slip the strap off my shoulders to get loose.

"Who's that?" I hear a guy say.

Then, Melanie, "That's Caitlin."

"Caitlin Madison?" asks a girl.

"Yeah."

"*Oh*," the guy says.

My face burns. I get my backpack loose and fight the urge to step back through the fence. Instead, I turn around and climb the bleachers.

"Close one," I hear myself say. My voice sounds different, but that's not entirely bad. Five skeptical faces turn to me. I keep talking. "Nails almost caught me ditching. I was walking straight toward him."

They don't say anything.

I set my backpack down next to a girl with a Metallica shirt that's so worn it must be a decade old.

"I'm gonna stay here for a few minutes. I really don't feel like having a chat with him right now." I say it so confidently that for a second it makes me feel confident, too, like I'm the kind of person who has near brushes with danger every day.

Then I sit down, and no one says anything. The Metallica girl bites a nail. The guy who asked about me earlier braids a chunk of his oily hair. I glance at Melanie—she's violently digging through her backpack. Two silent boys with glasses resume a card game.

"Shit," Melanie says. "Caitlin, do *you* have a cigarette?"

I assume that she's already asked everyone else there. I'm her last chance.

"Sorry," I tell her.

And for some reason, that breaks the ice.

"So, you were, like, best friends with Ingrid Bauer, right?" Metallica Girl asks.

"Yeah."

Oily-Hair Guy asks, "Did you know she was gonna do it? Like, did she tell you about it first?"

He says this like it's a completely normal question, like it's fine to ask people you don't know to tell you the details of the worst things that ever happened to them. It catches me off guard. I don't know how to react, so I just answer him.

"No."

"Too bad for you," says Metallica Girl.

The guy says, "I heard she slashed her wrists, right? That's awesome. It's not like just offing yourself with a gun or like carbon monoxide or something. Cutting yourself that fucking deep takes balls, you know?"

I open my mouth, but nothing comes out.

One of the cardplayers, still looking down at his cards, says, "My cousin's boyfriend threw himself off the Golden Gate Bridge, which is pretty sick, but I agree: it's easier than wrist slashing. You have to cut all the way through the tendon, you know. Most people get weak and pass out while they're doing it."

"What makes you such an expert?" Metallica Girl snaps.

"I was seriously considering doing it," the boy says, pushing up his glasses. "In eighth grade. I did a little research."

"You fucking loser," says the other cardplayer. "You fucking shithead loser. No one does *research*."

I have no idea who these people are. I look at Melanie. She's digging through Oily-Hair Boy's backpack now.

"Stop it," he whines.

The baseball field stretches in front of us—perfectly mowed lawn, neat brown mounds of dirt at the bases. I imagine myself walking to the middle of it and collapsing there. I see a scene play out like in those movies where they speed up time; where you see a plant sprout through dirt, bloom, and die in less than a minute. Except this time it moves backward. I fall asleep on the field; the blue sky turns gray then purple then black. The stars come out. The moon goes down. The sun rises. A year undoes itself. I move a little. I'm wearing different clothes, last year's clothes. The warning bell rings. I stand, reach for my backpack. It's lighter. I walk to first period, sit down next to Ingrid.

Melanie jumps to her feet, shattering my fantasy. She yells, *"I need a cigarette!"* And I have no idea what passed between us that day at the mall, because I don't feel anything now.

I don't want to hear another word that any of them say, so I lift my heavy backpack to my shoulders and start down the bleachers.

"See you later," I mumble, and manage to get through the fence without snagging anything. It isn't much of a victory, but at this moment it feels close.

3

Dylan isn't in class yet when I walk into English. I sit in my usual seat, get out the anthology, and force myself not to look up when people enter the room. They walk right past me, and I still keep my head down. Then I hear footsteps, and I know they're hers. She pauses right by my desk, probably waiting for me to look up. When I don't move, she sits behind me where she usually does.

"Hey," she says. "Where were you?"

She doesn't sound angry, and I realize that it isn't too late to turn back—I could think of some convincing excuse. I could say I'm sorry.

But I stay concentrated on the page. I don't even know what I'm looking at. Some poem. My eyes are so tired they won't focus on the words.

"I ran into some people," I say, and with that sentence, the damage is done.

"Who?" Dylan asks, now sounding pissed off.

"Just some people."

She doesn't say anything. I know that I should turn around and face her, but I don't.

Finally, I hear her mutter, "Whatever." The metal creaks as she leans back, hard, in her chair.

Soon Mr. Robertson comes in and starts lecturing. All through class Dylan swings her foot back and forth, kicking the leg of her desk with her boot, and even though I can hardly feel it, I want to flinch each time she makes contact.

The period passes agonizingly. As soon as the bell rings, Dylan grabs her stuff and storms out without looking back. I take my time getting to my locker, and by the time I make it to the science building, Dylan is gone.

4

Vista High School has tons of money, way more money than it could ever need. Because all the parents in Los Cerros are so rich, they're always writing checks to the school to fund the musicals, or the dances, or the smart kids' trips to Europe, where they tour museums by day and get drunk and go dancing at night. On one hand, it's pretty nice that we can have basically everything we want, but on the other, it makes me kind of uncomfortable. Amanda, Davey's fiancée, teaches history in the city and the books they use are so old that the covers have fallen off.

Sometimes, I feel a little guilty about all the stuff we have— our brand-new textbooks, the indoor swimming pool, the never-ending supply of photo paper and film. But at this moment I'm feeling pretty good about it all, because I'm hiding out in a shiny new bathroom that no one seems to know about yet. It seems completely unnecessary. It's between the math hall and the science hall, both of which also have bathrooms. But I'm not complaining. I'm sitting in an impossibly clean stall with the door shut, just in case someone comes in. Lunch is half over, and I'm a few pages into my treehouse book. It says that I'm going to need bolts, because nails and screws aren't strong enough.

On a piece of binder paper, I've sketched a plan. It's a view from the top of the tree, looking down. The trunk is in the middle, and around it is the floor—a hexagon. I'm not sure yet how long each side will be, or how wide, but I want it to be pretty big, not the kind of treehouse you feel like you have to get down and crawl around in. I want to be able to walk from side to side, to have an armchair in one corner, and a table with two more chairs against a wall. I know I want it to have lots of openings so daylight and air can come in. I'll have to think of a way to close the openings, though, in case it rains.

When the bell rings, and lunch is over, I decide to come back here tomorrow, and the next day, and the next. I tell myself it really isn't that bad.

5

Taylor and I sit on the soccer field, looking through one of the huge mathematician books he checked out from the library.

"This guy looks kind of cool," he says. "He was obsessed with clocks."

I'm trying to pay attention to what he's saying, but whenever I glance at the book I end up noticing how his eyelashes turn white at the tips. I keep forcing myself to resist touching them.

"Oh, crazy! This one guy went to prison for fraud!"

I reach over to grab one of the books and my knee presses against his. He doesn't pull away, doesn't even seem to notice. I feel my face getting hot. I open the book and try to focus. All I can do is wonder if Taylor knows that our knees are touching. I move mine away, just the tiniest bit.

Taylor and I already decided that we don't really care about finding a mathematician who discovered some amazing concept, we just want to find one who had an interesting life. I look down at the millimeter of space between Taylor's knee and mine, and start to read.

These books are full of boring information, like where certain mathematicians were born, and who they married, and what concepts they thought of and named after themselves. Then a word captures my attention: *pirate*.

"Hey, look at this," I say, and Taylor pushes his knee back against mine, leans closer until we're touching in so many places, puts his face so close to my face that I can feel him breathing, and starts to read where I point. I can tell that he's concentrating, but there's no way *I* can with him so close to me, so I glance up from the book for a second. Dylan is walking toward the parking lot with Marjorie Klein.

There are three kinds of outsiders at my school: the outsiders who everyone thinks are lame and nerdy, the outsiders who everyone looks at and thinks, *That kid looks* vaguely *familiar,* and the outsiders who are only outsiders because no one else is quite like them. Marjorie is the third kind, the best kind. Last year she tied with Ingrid for "most artistic."

Dylan and I haven't talked for over two weeks now. She's started sitting across the room from me in English, and ignores me whenever we're at our lockers together. Now she and Marjorie are gesturing like they're having this really great conversation, and I feel my body sink into the ground. Dylan says something and Marjorie laughs, and I wonder what great joke she made, and suddenly everything that was good about sitting here with Taylor is ruined. All I can think of is Dylan's boot kicking her desk, and the way she left class that day without looking at me.

"This guy looks awesome," Taylor's saying. "We should definitely choose this guy."

I look back down at the page. *Jacques DeSoir.*

"How cool is this," Taylor says. "A French renegade pirate mathematician."

Dylan and Marjorie are getting farther and farther away.

"I have to go," I say.

"Already?"

"My parents will want me home," I tell him, but really, I just need to get this image of Dylan and Marjorie out of my head.

"Want a ride?" Taylor asks.

"Okay," I say. "Thanks."

We head toward the parking lot, following far behind Dylan and Marjorie. Once we get there, I lose sight of them in the rows of cars.

"So we should have a map," Taylor says, "and, like, plot the course of Jacques DeSoir."

I nod and try to spot Marjorie's van. I wonder where they're going. I think of them at the noodle place, Marjorie ordering the most exotic thing on the menu, and I feel so replaceable.

Taylor and I stop. We're standing in front of his ancient, yellow Datsun hatchback. I haven't been paying attention to where we've been walking, and I realize that I'm standing by the driver's door and he's standing by the passenger's.

"Here!" Taylor says, and tosses a set keys over the car.

I catch them.

"You don't mind driving, do you?" he asks.

"Why?"

He grins and shrugs. "Unlock us?"

I do. I climb into the well-worn driver's seat, lean over to the passenger side, and pull the lock up. Taylor gets in. The inside of the car is warm and it smells like chocolate. We sit, looking at each other for a minute.

"I don't have my license."

"But you know how to drive, right?"

"Yeah."

"And you live nearby?"

"Right off of Oak."

"So that's not far."

"True," I say. "Not far at all."

"So I don't mind."

"Well, if you don't mind . . ." I say. I put the key in the ignition and the car spits and shakes to life. Taylor leans forward and rests his cheek against the dashboard. "Good, Datsun," he says. "Good little car."

I laugh at him and release the emergency brake. I wonder what the fuck I'm doing. If we got pulled over I could get arrested, I could lose the right to ever drive, I could get grounded for the rest of my high school life. But I can't stop myself. This is just happening. I'm just doing what I want to do and it feels good. I adjust the rearview mirror and see Marjorie's Volkswagen van pulling away from the sea of shiny, adult cars that kids around here get for their sixteenth birthdays: brand-new Accords and Passats and Maximas. I put Taylor's car in reverse.

"Careful when you switch to drive," Taylor says. "It gets kinda stuck sometimes."

I drive carefully out of the parking lot and down the street to the main road. It's a red light; I look for oncoming cars and then turn right. I expect Taylor to be all nervous that I'm behind the wheel, but he's leaning back in his seat, just smiling at me.

"You look good driving my car," he says.

We pass the hills and the strip mall and so many other cars. I glance at Taylor and find his eyes still on me. I've been so used to sitting still in the backseat that I've forgotten how much I liked the feeling of making a car move, take me somewhere. I'd forgotten how I called Ingrid one night after practicing for the test with my dad and told her, *This summer I'll drive us anywhere. Where do you want to go? Name a place and I'll drive us.*

At a stoplight, a car blaring hip-hop pulls up next to us.

A girl shouts, "Taylor!"

Alicia McIntosh is leaning out of her convertible Mustang.

He turns to me and rolls his eyes. The light turns green and he whispers, "Go!" I accelerate hard and Alicia's car gets smaller and smaller in the rearview mirror.

6

My parents say that I have an hour before dinner will be ready. I'm feeling too much to be in the house right now, so I go out to my car, but the space in there is too small to contain me. All through my chest and my stomach is this regret over what I'm doing with Dylan, in my hands and my feet is this electricity at the thought of Taylor leaning close to me, and all over my whole body, way, deep inside it, is this hurting over Ingrid. I could scream at the top of my lungs and the sound I would make wouldn't be half as loud as I'd need it to be.

An hour isn't a lot of time, but it's enough to do something, so I run across the backyard and down the hill and out to the oak tree and my pile of wood and box of tools and the bolts I bought. The treehouse book says that oak trees are perfect for treehouses, something about how their branches are shaped and angled. I've chosen to build the floor about ten feet up, in a spot where the branches aren't very dense.

First, I have to build myself a ladder.

I hoist up a long plank of wood and lean it against the tree. I pick out a handful of one-inch bolts and hammer them through the plank and into the tree trunk, spacing the bolts a foot apart from one another. The hammer feels heavy and solid in my hand. I can still feel recklessness in my stomach. As I work, I lose myself in memories of Ingrid.

The summer after ninth grade, Ingrid and I met two guys who went to a high school a few towns over. It was hot. We were bored. So we wandered the streets with them, ended up at a park they knew. We climbed through bushes and over rocks and ended up at a creek.

We sat with our feet in the water and listened to the friends talk about nothing, and laughed when we knew that something was supposed to be funny. Then, almost midconversation, the taller one leaned over to kiss Ingrid; and the other guy, as if on cue, pushed his mouth against mine. I jerked away—this wasn't what we had planned—and I was sure that Ingrid was going to also. But she didn't. The shorter one put his hand on my leg, but even that was too much, and soon I stood up and stepped deeper into the creek. He muttered something to his friend, and left. I looked into the water, up to the trees, over to where a stranger's hand inched up my best friend's shirt.

Later that night, she said, *God, Caitlin. We were only kissing.* It was true, but I kept thinking about how she felt about Jayson, and how this had been so different, so much less.

When I've hammered nails up one plank as high as I can reach, I line up another one about a foot away from the first and nail it to the tree. After that's done, I saw a piece off a third plank and bolt it in to make the first step. I look up through the branches and imagine what it will be like when the house is built and I'll sit in this tree and watch the sky turn black.

My dad calls me from the house. I've never felt an hour pass so quickly. I put my hammer back in the toolbox and close the metal lid. My arms are sore from lifting and pounding, but for some reason this makes me feel satisfied, like I really accomplished something. I walk back up the hill to my house, and wonder what Dylan is doing.

7

Ms. Delani is wearing a dress today. It's all black, sleeveless and billowy. She has a red scarf tied around her neck, and as she walks past me passing back work, her scarf trails behind her in the air. I watch the end of it swishing around. I want to reach out and yank it.

Then she stops in front of me, and drops a hideous, overexposed picture of dirt on my desk. My landscape. I flip it over. In thick red pen she's written *D*. Below it, *See me*.

Back in front of the classroom, Ms. Delani says, "Your next assignment is to take a self-portrait. Build off what you learned last year. And *please*," she says. "I want some depth. Some *substance*."

The bell rings and I slide to the edge of my chair. I don't want to *see* her.

I try to follow everyone out the door, but Ms. Delani catches me. "Caitlin."

I shuffle to her desk.

"Yeah?"

She reaches for the photo in my hand.

"Caitlin." She shakes her head. "What *is* this? This is not art."

I give her my iciest stare. "You didn't help me with my goals," I say. "I asked you, but you ignored me."

She sighs. "First a moving car for a still life. Now an empty lot for a landscape. I know that you are capable of much more than this."

I look away from her, up at the walls. I scan all the photographs until I find the one of me. "Actually, that was Ingrid," I say. "Ingrid was capable of more than this; I always sucked, remember?" I snatch my landscape from her, crush it in my fist, and shove it in my backpack.

She takes her glasses off and rubs between her eyes like I'm giving her the worst headache. She leans over her desk and puts her head in her hands. I stand there, awkwardly, waiting for her to look up and suggest that I drop the class, or tell me not to waste her time, or send me to the therapist again. I wait, and keep waiting. The freshmen start to come in for the beginning class. The bell for second period rings.

"Um," I say, shifting my weight from one foot to the other. "I kind of have to go." She still doesn't respond.

Then she sits up. And my heart stops beating. Ms. Delani's lips are trembling, her cheeks are flushed. She closes her eyes and tears run down and pool at the sides of her nose. She doesn't say anything. The freshmen are quiet, staring down at their desks, trying not to look at us. She reaches for a pad of paper and writes something. She hands me the paper and walks back into her office. I look down.

It says, *Please excuse Caitlin from second period tardiness. —V. Delani*

8

"So, hey," Taylor says as he's cramming his stuff into his backpack. "I'm going over to Henry's to wait for Jayson. We're gonna go to this kick-ass restaurant in Berkeley to get Ethiopian food. Wanna come?"

We've been comparing notes about Jacques DeSoir in the library after school. So far we've decided that we're going to start our presentation talking about how and why we chose him. We also decided to buy a map of Europe so that we can chart all the places he traveled for the class.

I feel kind of nervous about going to Henry's, but I also don't feel like saying no and walking home alone when I could be spending time with Taylor, so I say sure. Henry probably doesn't even know I exist, even though we're in English together and I know which block of which street he lives on. I know he lives in a three-story house and that his parents are never home. I know this because he has parties almost every Friday night, and because Ingrid and I would sometimes decide to go, get as far as the front yard, and then turn around when we saw the shapes of all the people inside, heard them talking and laughing, saw all the cars parked out front, and recognized whom they belonged to. Even though we wanted to go, we just couldn't bring ourselves to walk into Henry's house, see everyone already talking to people, already settled and gathered into little exclusive groups, and watch them look up at us and wonder why we were there.

So this is why I know the outside of Henry's house so well, but once I follow Taylor through the door, nothing is familiar. Not the huge family portrait that hangs in the entryway, not the marble floor, or the fountain that spurts water in the middle of it. I wonder what a kid does who lives here alone practically all the time. We turn into the family room.

Henry and a couple other guys I recognize but don't really know are sitting on an expensive-looking sofa, drinking Coronas and staring at the TV.

"Hey," Taylor says. "You all know Caitlin, right?"

One of them, not Henry, says, "Hey."

They all turn back to the screen. This is exactly what Ingrid and I feared all the times we turned around and walked away from Henry's house. I stand caught in this moment, feeling so unwelcome.

I would like to say that a million possibilities are running through my mind and that I'm just having trouble choosing which brilliant exit line to use, or which joke to deliver that will make all the guys laugh, make Taylor look less nervous, make the tension in the room vanish. But really, I'm just trying to think of one possibility. I'll do the first thing that comes to me. But before I've decided on anything, Henry speaks.

Still looking at the screen, he says, "Hey, so you're friends with that new girl, aren't you?"

I guess I was wrong; he does know I exist.

"Yeah," I say, and wonder if this is still true. I guess he really is oblivious if he hasn't noticed that Dylan and I haven't sat together for half a month.

He nods. "She's hot," he says. "Does she like guys, too?"

I shake my head, but realize that no one is looking at me, not even Taylor, who is studying his shoelaces as intently as he had been our Jacques DeSoir book. So I say it out loud: "I don't think so."

"Does she have a girlfriend?"

"Yeah," I say.

"Is *she* hot?"

"Um . . ." I roll up onto the balls of my feet and then back down. "It feels kind of weird to talk about this," I say.

"It's not a big deal," Henry says. "It's a simple question. So is she?"

"Taylor, I'm gonna wait outside," I say. I step outside and shut the heavy door behind me.

A second later, Taylor is beside me. "Sorry about in there," he says. "Henry's usually pretty cool."

"I'm sure he is," I say, kind of deadpan, and I don't know if Taylor can tell I'm being sarcastic. I'm so confused right now. I don't even want to work on the treehouse or fall asleep in my car. I don't even want Taylor to kiss me. The only thing that sounds remotely good is tracking Dylan down to tell her that I'm sorry about everything and that I understand I was being irrational and weird. A rumble comes from around the corner, and then a yellow Datsun appears with Jayson behind the wheel.

"Look, I'm gonna go," I say to the concrete.

"But you need to try this restaurant. It's really good, I swear. You won't be sorry."

"I'm just gonna go," I say.

Jayson slows and stops in front of us.

"At least let me drive you," Taylor says.

I raise a foot and step off the curb, pivot toward Taylor, and say, "I feel like walking." I manage a smile and add, "Thanks, though."

Taylor looks like a kid who didn't get what he wanted for Christmas.

I say, "If you have leftovers, you can bring me lunch tomorrow," and then I turn and head toward the strip mall.

I go into the noodle place. It smells like coconut milk and pineapple. Elvis is singing on the jukebox. Dylan isn't in there.

I decide to get some soup anyway. I sit in our usual booth and
eat alone.

9

I'm headed away from fourth period, when I feel a tap on my shoulder. It's Alicia, her red hair piled on top of her head in a huge mess.
I mean mess in a good way. Alicia always looks perfect.

"Caitlin," she says. "I'm glad I found you. I never see you at
lunch. Where do you sit?"

I can't really bring myself to tell her that I've been spending my
lunches hiding in bathroom stalls, so I shrug and say, "Different
places," and hope that it sounds vague in a cool way and not like
I'm too embarrassed to tell her the truth.

She doesn't seem too concerned with my answer anyway. Her
eyes are busy darting from side to side, like she doesn't really want
to be talking to me right now. Once she's convinced that no one
more important is around, she looks at me again.

"Listen," she says. "Caitlin."

She pauses like I'm supposed to say something.

"Um, yeah?"

She takes a breath and launches into her speech. "We've been
friends for so long. I mean a really, *really* long time. So I feel like it's
my responsibility to tell you that people are starting to say things
about you and that, um, *girl*."

"Dylan?"

She scrunches her nose and nods violently. "I mean, not that I
would ever believe them, but it's really something for you to think
about. I know that this is a hard time for you, and I'm just telling
you this because I care. I would just hate to see you fall in with the
wrong crowd."

I don't bother pointing out that one person does not really equal a crowd. I also don't mention that this advice is coming a little late.

"You have your reputation to consider," she concludes. And tilts her face. And smiles.

I look at each strand of red hair lacquered perfectly out of place, at her bright green eyes darting away from me to somewhere in the distance, and without thinking, I blurt out, "Alicia, do you consider yourself a shallow person?"

Alicia's attention jerks back to me. "*What?*" she asks.

"Because I don't consider myself a shallow person, either. But I think that people who make judgments about people they don't even know are shallow, and people who start rumors are shallow, and I really don't care about what shallow people say about me."

Alicia's eyes are open wide and fixed on my face. I can practically see her brain ticking. She says, "I'm just telling you for your own good. Because we've been friends since first grade. But now I see that you aren't grateful, so I'll stop caring. It'll make my life easier. So, thanks."

"No," I say, with my heart pounding and a brick in my stomach. "Thank *you*, Alicia."

Then I turn and walk away from her, toward the bathroom.

I stand in front of the mirror. I didn't turn in a self-portrait this morning. I didn't even take a bad one. Ms. Delani told us to turn them in at the end of class and I just grabbed my backpack and left as everyone was lining up to drop their photographs in the pile.

Behind me, on both sides, are long rows of empty bathroom stalls with silver doors. I lean over the sink, closer to my reflection, and stare at myself hard. I don't know what I see, I don't even know what I want to see.

Some days I like to think of myself as visibly wounded—like Melanie, only quieter. I imagine people wondering about what went wrong in my life. But other days I want to be like Dylan and

Maddy and their friends, who seem like they've lived a little, have been a little bad, but seem so healthy at the same time.

Really, when it comes down to it, I don't know if it's something I can decide. I back away from the mirror. I don't know what I see.

After school is over, I follow Dylan from English to the science hall. We turn our combination locks at the same time. I keep glancing over, trying to say hi, but she ignores me. A buzzing noise comes from her pocket and she reaches in and takes out her phone.

"Hey," she says to someone on the other end. "Yeah, I'm just leaving now." She slams her locker shut and walks out, still talking.

And I think how perfect this is, that the one time I actually speak up for myself, the one time I actually know what to say, it's over a nonexistent friendship.

I walk the back way home, fast, go straight to my room, unzip my backpack, and start reading. I need her.

DEAR RAIN CLOUDS,

you're lying so low over the ground, waiting to open up and
let the water spill out. i will put my red and black rain
boots on, the boots that i love but hardly ever get to
wear, throw gravel at caitlin's window and make her come
out to go stomp in puddles. we'll go down to the theater
and pick the lock, run up and down the aisles and just think
about who used to breathe in there. yesterday jayson told
me that he liked my hat. he said 'i like this' then he reached
out and tugged on one of the straps that hung down from
it, and i felt my whole body get soft. he smiled with his
teeth that are so impossibly white and straight. then when
the bell rang he stood up before me and he put his hand on
top of my head and said 'see you tomorrow.' i told caitlin.
i tried to drag the story out as much as i could so that
it could seem like a longer moment, so that it wouldn't end
with the telling of it. she grinned, said 'he totally loves
you.' and i just wanted to tell the story over, start from
the beginning. if we break into the theater i will lie on the
floor and talk to the ceiling, tell it everything i know about
jayson, ask the ceiling for advice, stare and stare and wait
for answers.

Love,
ingrid

By the time I'm finished reading I'm shaking. Everything gets blurry. I bury my head in my pillow, grab my comforter in both hands and try to rip it but nothing happens. I think about where she is now, in a coffin, underground in a cemetery I've only been to once and will never go to again. How it's so easy for her to not feel anything at all, to be just completely gone, to not be around to see how fucked up she's made me. She got to disappear completely and I feel like I'm about to combust. I stuff the corner of the blanket into my mouth until I can't fit any more of it in and then I scream and scream and the sound comes out muffled. And I wonder what was so bad that she couldn't do anything about it. What was so terrible that she felt she could never get over. When it gets too hard to breathe, I pull the blanket out and see that my teeth have only made little marks, tiny, invisible frays in the cotton. I can barely see them at all.

10

It's already getting dark when I wake up later that night, Ingrid's journal still open to the last entry I read. I can hear my parents downstairs making dinner. I have to clean my room—Taylor's coming over soon—but I'm hungry.

"Well, hey there, Sleeping Beauty," my dad says as I walk into the kitchen.

"Hey," I mumble.

My mom comes up to give me a hug, but I lean over to peer into the pantry and she goes back to the stove. I know it's mean of me, but I have this feeling that if I let her touch me, I would shatter into pieces.

"How was school?" my dad asks.

"Fine," I say.

I rummage through all the weird snacks my parents eat: dried apples, instant oatmeal, wheat crackers.

"Well," my dad says. "My day was fine, too. Thanks for asking. And let's hear how your mother's day was. Margaret?"

"It was nice, sweetheart," she says to my dad, but like she's really answering him, not trying to give me a lesson in social etiquette.

I find a bag of pretzels and tear it open, put one in my mouth, and taste the salt. My mom glances over at me. "Honey, have you been crying?" she asks.

I stare at the food she's making and shrug.

"Taylor's coming over to work on our project for precalc," I say. "So I'm not going to be able to eat with you guys."

"Can't he come over after dinner?" my dad asks.

"This is important," I say. "You know it's, like, for school?"

"Well, he's welcome to join us."

"Uh, no thanks."

"Why were you crying?" my mom asks. "Are you okay?"

"I just had a bad day. Is that not allowed?" I say, and it comes out a little harsher than I meant it to. I turn away and start heading back up to my room with the pretzels. On my way out I grab a Popsicle from the freezer.

At eight-fifteen, the doorbell rings and I rush past my parents to let Taylor in. He looks around nervously and catches sight of my parents. They are sitting at the dining table, eating something that smells really good.

"I'm sorry to interrupt your dinner," he says to them.

He's carrying his backpack and his skateboard, but it's clear that he's tried to make himself look nice. He smells like shampoo.

"We're having penne and a beet salad," Mom says. "May we offer you some?"

"Thanks, but I already ate," Taylor says, taking off his jacket.

"We can go upstairs now," I say.

"Okay, great. I brought the map and those little pushpin things."

We start to walk away when my dad calls out, "That's a nice shirt you have on, Taylor."

It's just a plain T-shirt, solid green.

Taylor's whole face turns red. "Um, thank you," he stammers. He pauses, then adds, "Sir."

Once my door is closed, he says, "Oh my God. Your dad totally hates me. He thinks I'm trouble. I knew I should never have bought that stupid sex shirt. I knew it was a stupid thing to do."

"You should get a new one," I say. "One that says something like 'Will work for forgiveness.'"

"Or 'redemption.'"

"Or 'approval.'"

He smiles. "Think it would work?" he asks.

"Maybe."

"Should I make the effort?"

He's standing close to me; his breath smells minty, I can't concentrate, so I say, again, "Maybe."

We both stand there, not knowing what to say or do next, until Taylor sets his backpack down and starts taking stuff out. I sit down on the chair by my desk. I get up and sit on my bed. I get up again, and plant myself, cross-legged, on the carpet.

Taylor has already taken out everything we need to get started, but he doesn't stop there. Soon pencils and paper napkins and paper clips and books for other classes form a small mountain beside him.

"Looking for something?" I ask.

"What? Oh. No, just taking inventory." He dumps it all back in. Once everything is packed up again, he looks at all the stuff on my walls.

"Nice room," he says.

And then, a second later, he says, "Oh." It comes out kind of shocked, like it wasn't something he meant to say. I look at him, then up to where he's looking. It's a picture of Ingrid tacked up on my wall. She looks pretty, standing on the grass by the reservoir smiling.

"You must miss her a lot."

I can't say anything. I pick at the carpet.

"If you don't want to talk about it, it's okay."

I keep picking at the carpet, hoping that I won't start crying again.

Taylor slides a rubber band off the map he brought and spreads the map out across the space between us.

"Okay," he says. "So this is Nice, where Jacques DeSoir grew up. We should put the first thumbtack here. Where was the next place he went? I'll look it up."

He opens the book and flips through the pages. I don't want to talk about geography; I just want to be close to someone. I know that I'm only a couple feet away from him. I know that my parents are only a staircase away.

But still, I feel alone.

Silently, I pull my shirt over my head.

My heart is beating in my throat.

Still staring at the book, he says, "Okay, so it looks like he went to these Greek Islands." No boy has seen me in just a bra before. I wait for him to look up.

Then he does.

His face flushes and he swallows slowly. I ease forward, across a thousand pastel-colored countries and into his lap, wrap my legs around his waist, and kiss him.

His mouth feels cold and my tongue grazes his mint gum. He touches my back with warm hands and I wonder if he's fantasized about something like this, if he's ever thought of me like this before. I hope he has, because I'm not really this brave. We kiss and kiss. I wait for him to start fumbling with my bra strap like boys in movies do, but he doesn't. His hands move across my back gently and I still feel far away. I still feel alone. I start hearing these words

in my head. *i want you to touch me. i want you to take my clothes off.*
I hear them over and over, like the chorus of a song, before I realize that they're Ingrid's words, that I'm feeling what Ingrid felt, and
it's then I start to panic. I don't stop kissing Taylor. I don't stop
anything. I don't know what I'll do when this moment is over and
I'll actually have to see him look at me.

But then it happens.

Taylor's body gets tense. He stops kissing me. I climb off of him.
I sit. I cover my chest with my arm. I look at his sneakers, at the
frays on the bottom of his jeans, anywhere but at his face. I look at
his hand as it moves to where my tank top lies on the carpet and as
he lifts it up for me to take. I put it back on.

We sit in silence.

Then Taylor says, "I should go."

I close my eyes. I'm waiting for the world to end.

I nod, whisper, "Okay."

There's the sound of him putting his books back into his backpack, of him rolling up the map. The sound of a zipper zipping.
The sound of him standing up. The silence of his not moving.

"I'll see you tomorrow," he says.

I open my eyes and scan the ceiling. "Okay."

He walks softly out of my room. I watch the back of him as he
eases the door closed. Once it's shut, I lean forward and put my
head in my hands. Then the door swings open again, and Taylor
comes back. He leans against my wall and says, "Just so you know,
I do like you. That just felt weird."

I guess I should say something, but I don't. At this moment I am
so far from thinking clearly, so far from making sense.

"Caitlin?" he asks.

I look into his face for the first time in minutes.

"I just want to make sure you know. It's not like I didn't want it
or anything."

He waits for me to say something. When I don't, he walks in from the doorway and kneels on the carpet next to me. I get this terrible feeling that he's going to kiss my cheek out of pity. I put my hand over my face so he can't get to it.

"You know," he says, "I had this huge crush on you in third grade."

"Third grade?" I don't even remember knowing him in third grade.

"Yeah, Mrs. Capelli's class. Remember?"

I move my hand away from my face. I do remember. Mrs. Capelli wore colorful sweaters that smelled like mothballs and kept a hamster as the class pet.

"Your desk was one row ahead of mine and one row over, which was like the best setup imaginable because I could stare at you all day long without you seeing me."

I glance at him and try to remember what he looked like as a little kid. I can remember him from middle school, practicing skating tricks in the front circle after the bell rang, but I can't visualize him as an eight-year-old.

I open my mouth to ask him a question, then think better of it.

"What?" he asks.

So I say it anyway. "What did you like about me?"

"Lots of things." He shifts his weight and ends up a little closer to me—still not touching, but closer. "But what I remember the most is this thing you used to do whenever we did art projects."

"What was it?"

"Okay, well, you know how we had those boxes at our desks with our names on them? You kept a plastic bag in one—not a grocery bag, it was more like a sandwich bag. So, I'd glance over at you a lot during art projects and watch you gluing things. You always worked really slowly and carefully, and you hardly ever finished anything."

I nod. It's true—the art hour was always too short.

"So when Mrs. Capelli would tell us that our time was up, most of the kids just dumped the colored-paper scraps and glitter and cotton balls and stuff into the trash, but you would get out your plastic bag and put everything you didn't use inside it."

I haven't thought about that for years, but as he says it, I remember. I can see myself, my little-kid fingers putting everything into that bag, saving it for later.

"Popsicle sticks and those pipe-cleaner things . . . I mean, it was *junk,* but you'd put it in your bag with glitter and suddenly it would look special. It used to drive me crazy."

He grins, and even though my heart is lodged permanently in my throat, I smile back.

"I mean crazy in a good way," he adds. He stands up. "Okay, I'm really going now. See you tomorrow."

Once I hear him descend the stairs and shut the front door, I get up and look in my closet for my third-grade yearbook. It only takes a minute to find. I stick it in my backpack.

"I'll be outside," I yell, so my parents won't panic if they can't find me later.

In the garage, I find my dad's huge flashlight that he uses on his search-and-rescue trips. I turn it on and head down the hill, out to my oak tree. So far, I've built a ladder ten feet up and secured six spokes to the trunk, one for each wall of the treehouse. I balance the flashlight on a branch above my head, stuff some bolts in my pocket, grab my hammer, and haul up a plank of wood. Once I'm up, I straddle a branch and prop one end of the plank onto a step, and attach the other end to the end of a spoke so that they form a forty-five-degree angle. This new plank will be the first brace, and I need to attach six of them to support the six spokes. I keep my mind clear, focus on the sound of my hammer and the weight of the planks.

Once I've secured half of them, my arms feel weak. I'm determined to get all six up tonight, though, so I'll just give myself a short break.

I ease my way to the ladder and climb down. I take the yearbook out of my backpack. The flashlight casts a glow all around me—on the tree trunk, the grass, the leaves on the ground, the twigs and the pebbles. If I could, I would collect everything about right now. It's not that I'm happy. I'm embarrassed and confused and so mad at myself about Dylan. But there's something about right now that feels good despite everything. Each time a breeze starts, I feel the air all the way through me.

I flip through the yearbook pages until I find Mrs. Capelli's class. There, in the lower right corner, is Taylor's picture—small, black-and-white, grainy, but still incredibly charming. He's smiling this bright, open smile. Even then he looked like a kid from a movie, the kind who only has a couple lines and can't even remotely act, but no one cares because he's so cute. I find my own picture. I'm smiling shyly with my hair in barrettes, my face slightly tilted to one side. This was me before I knew about anything hard, when my whole life was packed lunches and art projects and spelling quizzes. When my biggest responsibility was the one weekend of the year when it was my turn to bring the class hamster to my house and make sure it had food and water.

I move the flashlight closer, and study my eight-year-old face again. I change my mind. I was such a quiet kid, so shy and calm and in my own head. Of course I knew about being sad. Maybe that's the reason I saved all the things I thought were pretty.

After I've put up two more braces, I realize I'm stuck. There's no way for me to attach the sixth brace to the sixth beam; the branches around it are either all too high or too low. It's more than I can do tonight. Soon I'll climb farther up and secure a rope to a high branch. I'll make a swing so I can reach the places I can't reach yet.

11

I know I should eat something, but my stomach is still messed up over what happened with Taylor last night. I fill a spoon with cereal, then lower it back into the bowl. My parents are reading the paper at the table in the kitchen, and when my dad gets up to get his briefcase from the other room, my mom clears her throat and turns to me.

"Caitlin," she says in her school-principal voice, "I'm glad to see that you're spending some time with new people. It's important for you to make new friends. I do want to ask, though—and this isn't a big deal, it's just something your dad and I decided—that I'd like you to keep your door open when you have Taylor over. Or any boy. It doesn't have to be wide open, just open a little."

I stare at my cranberry-almond crunch getting soggy in the milk.

"Why?"

My mom's newspaper rustles. "It's just the appropriate thing to do. We trust you, we just also know what it's like to be your age. It's fine for you and Taylor to enjoy each other's company." She pauses. "It's even fine to kiss, or *make out,* or whatever you want to call it. Just as long as you keep the door open to keep you from getting carried away."

I feel this pinch in my gut and, for a brief moment, I want to tell my mom what I did, but the feeling leaves immediately.

Instead I say, "My friend Dylan's a lesbian, so do I have to leave the door open when she's over, too?" It comes out all snappy, and I feel kind of bad, because my mom's obviously trying to be nice about this.

She sighs. "Well, honey, are *you* a lesbian?"

"No."

"Well, then I think you can leave the door closed."

"Okay," I say, trying to sound kinder. "Sounds fair."

12

I can't go to precalc. I've tried all morning to gather the courage, but there is no possible way I can face Taylor right now.

When second period ends I go up to my locker. A few minutes pass and then the bell for third period rings and everyone disappears from the hallways. I swing my locker door back and forth. I stare at Ingrid's picture and wonder if I could find that hill again. I head down to the bathroom.

I push open the door and walk in, expecting it to be empty as usual. But it's not. Dylan's in there, standing right in front of me with her back turned, washing her hands at the sink. She startles when I walk in, and I feel like I'm seeing a ghost. The fluorescent lights on the ceiling make everything blue.

"What are you doing here?" I ask her.

There's something about seeing her so unexpectedly that makes me look closer. Still standing behind her, by the door, I look into the mirror at the sharp line of her jaw, the way her collarbone juts out over her chest, a tiny scar on her forehead that I never noticed before.

She looks at my reflection, says, "I wasn't aware that you owned the bathroom."

In this light, her skin looks so pale against all her black clothes. The water rushes in the sink then stops. Dylan rips a paper towel off the roll. She turns, stuffs the towel in the trash, and thumps past me out the door. Even after she's left, I don't move. The school year is almost half over. I wonder if there is any way I can get her to forgive me.

That night, before I go to sleep, I open my window and lean with my camera into the night sky. I set the shutter speed fast so if there's any trace of light the camera won't see it. I snap the picture.

Our next assignment is about contrast. I will be turning in a perfectly black photograph.

13

On Saturday morning, I wake up remembering how Ingrid and I used to spend the weekends taking pictures. We'd go to all the same places, hardly talking, in search of perfect shots. Then we'd sneak into the darkroom together and develop everything.

There our day would be: my version drying on one line, Ingrid's drying across the room. I'd look at all her images from my day and I wouldn't recognize them. The mall lobby: I saw a meager bunch of balloons in the entrance of a new store; she saw an empty stroller. My room: I saw a pile of magazines on the carpet; she saw a note from my mom that said, *Remember laundry.* A park in San Francisco: me, seagulls in flight; her, a hill with grass and wildflowers.

I miss that feeling of dropping the exposed paper into the chemical bath, holding my breath for a moment, then seeing the image take shape. The dark parts darkening. Thinking, *I* made *this.*

I have a black photo to develop, but I also want that feeling back. I want to make something to hang on my wall after it dries. I dig through my drawer to find the roll of film I shot the night before junior year started. I don't expect that the moon photographs will come out, but the one of my house might.

I hoist myself through the photo-lab window and head straight into the darkroom. As soon as I round the corner to where the sinks are, I can feel that something is different: I am not alone.

I wait for my eyes to adjust.

At first I don't recognize her. She's in jeans and a hoodie, her hair swept back in a ponytail. She stands with her back to me, hanging a photograph.

"Hello, Caitlin," Ms. Delani says.

"Hey," I mutter, and brace myself to be thrown out.

But she doesn't lecture me on breaking and entering or threaten to call my parents. Instead, she says, "The enlarger in the corner is free."

"Okay."

Hesitantly, I feel my way to the enlarger. Her safety light is on, though, so I can't pop open my film canister yet. Even the dimmest light could expose it too soon. I don't want to ask her to turn off her light for me, but it would seem rude if I just left after she told me I could stay. I wait, motionless, trying to figure out what to do.

"Are you developing?" she asks.

"Yeah," I say.

She flips off her light.

"Thanks."

I hurry to loop my film around the reel and twist on the top so no light will seep through.

"Finished," I say, and her light clicks back on. I try to catch a glimpse of her developed photographs, soaking in water. They are all of motels illuminated by "Vacancy" signs.

For a little while it's like nothing is wrong between us. We work in silence, side by side. I'm testing my exposure on a contact sheet; she's making print after print, so confidently.

When she packs up to go, I assume I won't be able to stay here without her. I gather my negatives. I haven't even gotten to see what my house photograph will look like.

But then she says, "Shut the window tightly when you leave. It's supposed to rain tonight."

14

Sunday, 8 A.M.

I wake up, stomach sinking. Still half asleep, I reach under my bed for Ingrid's journal. I put it next to me on the pillow, rest my hand on the smooth, cool cover, and fall back to sleep.

8:27.

I open my eyes and open to the first page. Ingrid's drawing of herself stares up at me. I fall into a silent dream of her swinging in the park, head thrown back in laughter. What was it we were laughing about?

9 A.M.

I pull back the covers and get out of bed.

At ten, I get out of the shower and wrap myself in a towel. After rummaging through my desk drawer, I finally find my school directory. I find Jayson's number, pick up the phone, and dial.

My heart feels like a hummingbird.

"'Lo?" says a guy's voice.

"Hi, is this Jayson?"

"Yeah, who's this?"

"This is Caitlin," I say. I consider saying my last name, since I'm not exactly the first person Jayson would expect to call him at ten-fifteen on a weekend morning.

But before I can decide, he says, "Hey, Caitlin. What's up?" He says it nicely, like it's a surprise that I'm calling, but not an unpleasant one.

"I'm wondering if you might want to grab a cup of coffee," I say.

"Sure," he says. "When?"

"Like, in an hour?"

"An hour?"

"Is that too soon?"

He pauses. "No," he says. "I could probably swing that."

I get dressed and brush my teeth and leave a note for my parents, who are nowhere to be seen. I find my mom's bike in the garage and hop on it; I put on her helmet even though it looks nerdy. I am not the most confident rider.

The streets are quiet this morning. I ride past the park and the fire station. When I turn the corner, I see Jayson leaning against the front of the café. He lifts a hand in my direction. I ride up to him and climb off the bike.

"Hey," I say.

"Hey," he says.

We smile.

"You want coffee?" I ask.

"Coffee stunts your growth."

"You should tell Dylan that." I laugh.

"She's seriously addicted, isn't she? I mean, I don't really know her, but it's like she has a coffee cup permanently attached to her hand."

"Very true. But she's tall enough already," I say, relieved that we're having a conversation instead of an awkward silence while he wonders why he's here. "Hot chocolate?" I try.

He makes a face. "I'll find something."

I lock my bike to a parking meter and we walk through the café door. It chimes as we go in. I order a mocha with whipped cream and Jayson ends up getting green tea.

"For here or to go?" the woman at the cash register asks.

Jayson looks at me for the answer.

"To go," I say.

When we get back outside, Jayson finally asks what this is about. "Not to be rude," he says. "I'm just curious."

"Today is Ingrid's birthday." I stop breathing for a moment, fully aware that this is the first time that we've ever talked about Ingrid as being something between us. "I needed someone to celebrate with, and I don't know if you knew or not, but she was pretty in love with you."

His smile vanishes, and without thinking at all, I reach out and put my finger on the line that forms between his eyebrows.

He doesn't flinch when I touch him, but the line stays there even after I take my hand away. Finally, he says, "I kept waiting for something to happen with us. It was just weird, you know, 'cause she wasn't in my group of friends or anything. And things were kind of going on with another girl who liked me, and everyone knew and expected me to like her, too. So I was just kind of . . . I was just waiting for things to figure themselves out, you know? And then Ingrid was just gone one day. I mean, it was horrible, everyone thought it was horrible, but for me it was like . . ."

I wait for him to finish, but he just shakes his head back and forth.

"Let's go," I say. And I have him hold my mocha in one hand and his tea in the other as I walk my mom's bike toward the theater. As we're walking, Jayson keeps trying to explain.

He says, "Everyone was really shocked. Well, you know they were shocked."

"No," I say. "I don't know how anyone felt. After the morning it happened, I never went back to school. I missed finals week, and by the time this year started, hardly anyone said anything about it."

"Oh," he says. "Well, they were. Everyone was sitting around wondering what happened, saying how they never would have expected it, how she was so talented, and they wished they knew her better. Stuff like that."

I think about this. I try to picture it. I want to ask Jayson, *Who? Who was saying that?* I want him to give me names, because it's so hard for me to imagine. It's not that Ingrid was unpopular, it's just that we mostly kept to ourselves.

We keep walking and soon the street turns to gravel and the cars stop passing, and it's just Jayson and me by the theater.

He turns to me and says, "I listened to everyone else talking, and I kept thinking that it was different for me. I mean, I felt like we were gonna have something . . . something was gonna happen for us one of those days. I thought about her all the time. I mean, *all the time*. She was just adorable. I *knew* that we were gonna be a thing one day. I was just waiting for things with Anna to blow over and then Ingrid *died*. And everyone was talking about her and I felt like telling everyone that it was different for me, but I knew that was stupid. I didn't deserve it."

I know that if I could think of the right thing to say, I could make him feel so much better. I try to think of myself, of all the things I need to hear, and then I think of how it used to be when I talked to Dylan. Maybe there is no right thing to say. Maybe the right thing is just a myth, not really out there at all.

I lean my bike against the ticket booth and head around the corner, Jayson's footsteps behind me. When I get to the back, I try to open the door, but, as always, the old brass doorknob won't turn. I try the single skinny window. Sealed shut.

I look at the ground and find a rock the size of my fist.

"What are you doing?" Jayson asks.

What *am* I doing?

I look at him and shrug.

Then I smash in the window. The glass shatters and I get a shard stuck in my fingertip.

"Shit!" I say, pulling it out. It starts to bleed and I stick it in my mouth.

Jayson stands a few feet away from me, staring like I'm crazy.

"Hold on," I say. I kick the rest of the glass in and push the drape aside. Then, careful to avoid the remaining glass, I step in.

Inside is cool and dark. It smells musty and familiar, like the science hall, like my grandparents' garage. I stand for a moment and let my eyes adjust to the dark. When I can see well enough, I try to open the door, but it must have been locked from the inside with a key. I go back to the window.

"I can't open it," I say to Jayson. "You'll have to come in this way."

Jayson looks hesitant, but eventually swings a leg over to join me. We stand next to each other with our backs to the wall and take in what's in front of us. It's a small room with a tattered couch and a couple lockers and a coat hanger. A ladder rests against one of the walls.

"This must have been the break room," Jayson says.

The break room leads to the lobby and its empty concession stand. The ceiling is higher than I had pictured, the dusty floor is tiled in gold, green, and blue, and the doors to the screening room are wide open and welcoming, as if a film is just about to start.

Jayson and I walk to the top of the aisle and look down at all the empty red velvet seats and the blank screen.

"Ingrid and I used to come around here all the time," I say. "It was our favorite place to hang out."

Jayson turns to me. "You guys used to hang out here?" he asks.

I nod.

"This is crazy," he says. "Every night I go running, and half the time I run by here. I always thought it was so cool, and I kind of thought that no one knew about it but me."

"We thought that nobody knew about it but us," I say.

He shakes his head. "I can't believe it's gonna be torn down."

Jayson and I stay in the theater for a while, exploring. We find a cracked mug and a file of index cards listing the titles, directors, and running times of hundreds of films. We find the long narrow staircase to the projection room. Up there we find an umbrella, boxes and boxes of old film reels, a bag of black letters for the marquee, and a man's hat. When our eyes begin to ache from straining to see in the dark, Jayson climbs out of the window and I climb out after him.

We walk back toward the coffee shop without talking. When we get there, Jayson stops in front of his dad's car. "Do you want a ride home?" he asks.

"No," I say. "I have my bike."

He opens the car door but doesn't climb inside.

"So, does Taylor think I'm a complete loser?" I ask.

Jayson looks at me, alarmed.

I roll my eyes. "I'm *sure* he told you all about the other day."

"He didn't tell me anything," he says, but I can tell he's lying.

"I'm sure," I repeat.

He doesn't say anything for a second and then he laughs. "Okay, he told me. But we're best friends, you know, so don't go thinking that everybody knows. It's just me."

I look down at the concrete. "I'm so embarrassed," I say. "I don't know why I did that."

Jayson grins. "Don't take this the wrong way or anything," he says. "But it all sounded pretty hot to me."

"Well, thanks." I laugh. "Thanks so much."

"No. But seriously, Taylor totally likes you."

"Okay," I say.

"So don't worry."

I get on my mom's bike. "Okay. I'm not worried."

Jayson lifts his hand good-bye. I lift mine back.

"Thanks," he says, "for everything."

"No problem," I say, and head back home.

15

Later that day, I head to Dylan's house.

When I get to her gate, she's walking out the door in a gray jump-suit that makes her look like a fashionable gas-station attendant.

"Oh," I say. "Are you leaving?"

She glances at me. "I'm on my way to the post office."

"But it's Sunday. The post office is closed."

"I'm just using the stamp machine."

"Can I walk with you?"

She looks up at the sky and squints, pushes her rolled-up sleeves over her elbows, shrugs, and starts walking.

I follow her. We get to the end of her street and turn before I manage to make myself tell her that I'm sorry.

"I'm kind of working through a lot of stuff right now, but I shouldn't have taken it out on you."

"That's true," she says. "You shouldn't have."

"Well, I'm sorry," I say.

We keep walking, and then suddenly we're by the empty lot where I took my landscape, except it's not empty anymore. The bones of a house are coming up.

"Hey, look," I say.

Dylan glances at the house. "Yeah," she says. "The owners already booked my mom to cater their housewarming party."

"I wonder how it'll look when it's finished."

We start walking again.

"So, nice work on the treehouse," Dylan says. "You're making progress."

"Oh my God. Stalker!"

Dylan laughs. "I had to ask you a question, so I went over to your house, but no one was home. I knew you were building one, so I walked down the hill and found it. Your parents have a ton of property."

"What did you want to ask me?"

"Actually, it was Maddy who wanted me to ask you," Dylan says. "She has the lead in a play. She's a really great actor, you know. Anyway, she wants you to come. I don't know if it's such a great idea."

My stomach sinks. Maybe I really have ruined our friendship for good. "Why not?"

"The play is *Romeo and Juliet*. I didn't know if that's something you'd really like to see right now."

"Oh," I say, but I'm not sure what she means.

We cross the street to the strip mall and head toward the post office. Dylan pauses outside the glass doors. "I'll just be a second."

I walk over to a pole and lean against it. Why would Dylan think

I wouldn't want to see *Romeo and Juliet*? I'm pretty good at English. It's not like Shakespeare's over my head or anything. We read it freshman year. Actually, I think I can recite a few lines. I try to remember the different parts I know—the balcony scene, the part with Juliet and the nurse, the part when she realizes that Romeo drank all the poison . . . *Oh.*

Dylan comes back out and sits on the curb.

"Today is Ingrid's birthday," I tell her. "She would have been seventeen."

Dylan remains quiet, and even though I'm close to tears, I smile. Here she is, once again, never saying things just to say them.

"I'd like to go to the play. When is it?"

"Friday."

"We'll go over together?"

Dylan shrugs. "I don't know." She hugs her knees to her chest. I want to ask her a million questions about her life, but I don't think it's the right time.

She smirks. "So what have you been doing lately? Just running into people?"

"Mostly hiding in the bathroom, actually."

"Sounds lovely."

"Well, it's a really nice bathroom. Oh, and you know Taylor Riley?"

"Yeah, he's in my chemistry class."

"I kissed him."

She stretches her legs out in front of her. "Oh yeah? Good for you."

"No," I say. "I mean I threw myself at him. I mean I took off my shirt and attacked him."

Dylan squints up at me. I can't tell what she's thinking.

"It was undoubtedly the most humiliating moment of my life."

Dylan keeps squinting and then smiles wide.

"I'm sorry," she says, "I know it's not funny, I'm sorry. But *why*?"

"I don't know. I was just lonely, I guess." I peel a strip off an old flyer stapled to the pole, advertising a garage sale that happened last weekend. I stuff the strip into my hand and peel another.

I try again: "So, we'll go over together, right? On Friday?"

I don't look at Dylan, just peel off another strip. It says HOUSEHOLD APPLIANCES! FURNITURE! KNICK-KNACKS! I wait for her to answer.

She doesn't say anything.

I pry a staple out of the wood.

"I really want to see Maddy act," I say.

I try to remember what Maddy said about the light, the aura. I crumple the paper into a ball and put it in my pocket.

Finally, Dylan sighs. "Look," she says. "I don't want to make a huge thing out of this, but I like to be direct about things. I don't know what happened to you at lunch that day, but I have a feeling that it had to do with Ingrid. So, I just want to make this clear: I'm not a replacement for her. If you're trying to make that happen, our friendship isn't going to work. It's not what I want, and it shouldn't be what you want, either."

I sit down next to her. She's looking at me in the way only she can, with all this intensity, not self-conscious at all.

"That's not what I want," I say. Dylan doesn't respond, so I know I have to try harder.

"Remember that day when I showed you the theater?" I ask.

"Yeah."

"You told me that you chose me to be your friend."

"*Okay,*" she says, half defensive, half embarrassed.

"Well," I say. "It's my turn. I choose you."

"What?"

"I choose you. You're my friend now. If I have to stalk you at your locker and, like, *beg* you to go eat with me after school, and trespass in your backyard, I will."

Dylan rolls her eyes, but when she smiles, her intensity fades into something warmer. "Fine."

"So we'll eat lunch together tomorrow. Preferably not in the bathroom, because even though it's really nice in there, I could use a change of scene."

"But wait," Dylan says, all sarcastically. "If memory serves me correctly, school bathrooms are some of my favorite places."

"If Maddy comes out here one day, you guys can make out in there all you want, but I'd like to eat on the soccer field."

"Okay, fair." Dylan nods.

"And we're going to the play on Friday."

"Fine, but you should ask Taylor because Maddy and I are going to want to hang out after."

"Oh." I nod knowingly. "*Hang out.*"

"You may need to be entertained."

"Okay," I say.

"Okay." She nods. "Good."

16

After dinner on Sunday night, the phone rings.

"Hello, is this Caitlin?" a woman asks.

"Yeah?"

"Caitlin, this is Veena."

The phone suddenly seems heavy.

"Veena Delani."

"Oh," I manage. "Hi."

"I wonder if I could schedule a meeting with you for Monday. Before class, or during break. There's something I'd like to discuss with you."

"I'm sorry about sneaking in," I say. "I won't do it anymore."

"That's not what I want to meet with you about."

"Oh," I say. "Well, I didn't want to look at myself like that."

"Sorry?" she asks.

"That's why I didn't turn in a self-portrait."

She says, "Yes, I had noticed that you missed the assignment. To be honest, I'm worried about your standing in the class in general."

I don't really know what to say to that, so I don't say anything.

"So, when can you meet?"

"I guess before class would work," I say.

"Seven-thirty?"

"Okay."

I hang up the phone. I stand in my room and look at my walls, at the picture of Ingrid by the reservoir, at all the magazine ads I cut out because I thought the photography was amazing.

17

When I walk into advanced photo early Monday morning, Ms. Delani looks up from her desk and actually smiles.

I want to say, *Just tell me, just get it over with: I'm actually going to fail photography.*

She gestures to the chair on the other side of her desk. I do as told, and sit.

She says, "Caitlin, we've gotten off to a rough start this year, haven't we?"

I shrug. She's looking at me, patiently. I'm starting to wonder where this conversation will go.

"To be honest, I was hoping that you wouldn't take my class again." Her eyes are intent behind her thin-framed, red glasses, and as her words register I feel completely numb, like all my blood is being replaced with ice. There isn't anything I can say to her. I want to disappear.

"Have you ever wanted to be a teacher?" she asks casually, as if she hasn't just ripped my heart out.

I manage to shake my head no. I don't know if I will ever speak again.

She leans back in her chair. I want her to stop looking at me. I want to sink into the floor, find somewhere dark and cold, and never come out.

"As a teacher, you dream of finding the perfect student, the most promising student." I stare at the floor and nod. "It's partially selfish, really. We, as teachers, like to think that we play an integral role in our students' development. We dream of being that one teacher that people remember all their lives, the one who inspired them to achieve great things."

I keep nodding.

"I found that student in Ingrid."

I stop.

"Then I lost her."

I feel like dirt. My face burns.

"I'll drop the class if you want me to. I can transfer into study hall."

She shakes her head. She says, "Let me finish. I was lucky. I found *two* students."

She's leaning on her desk toward me. "The other one was you."

"Yeah, right," I say. "You think my work is shit."

"Why would you say that?"

"Just look up," I say. "You stuck my picture in the corner, as out of the way as possible."

"I see that my lesson on how the eye moves through a piece of art wasn't very memorable," she says. "When someone looks at something, the eye is immediately drawn to the top left corner. Ingrid's three photographs are in the center because they are the most complex and evocative. I wanted people to linger on them. But yours is in the left corner because it is immediately striking, and I wanted people to see it first when they walked into the classroom."

This lesson sounds vaguely familiar, but I still don't know if I believe her.

"Ingrid's natural talent surpassed that of any student I've ever had. She turned photographs in to me all the time, almost every day, photographs that weren't even assigned. She had passion, ambition. I was certain that she would make it in the art world." I want to say, *So was I,* but Ms. Delani doesn't pause long enough to let me.

"But you," she says. "You are growing so much. Even though you don't want me to see it. I went back to the darkroom on Saturday, after you'd gone. I saw the print you left drying. That was excellent work, Caitlin. Not only was it technically impressive— that you could capture the house at night, show the darkness without compromising the detail—but it told a story. In the dead of night, two lights are on in a house. In a window, a woman's silhouette. It makes me wonder what is happening in that house, why the woman isn't sleeping, who is taking the photograph, why she isn't inside . . .

"Stay here," she says, and retreats into her back office. She comes out carrying a large frame. I can only see the back.

"I don't know if Ingrid told you, but I convinced her to enter a national student photography contest. It was only a few weeks before she took her life."

"No," I say. "I didn't know that," and as I say it I feel flooded with bitterness at all the things Ingrid kept secret from me.

"She had gathered somewhere that judges look down at portraits, that it's considered more artistic not to photograph people, so at first she submitted that sweet shot of the hill. I like that photograph; I don't think it's her *strongest* image, but I like it. Anyway, on the morning of the deadline, she changed her mind and came to me with this."

Ms. Delani lifts the frame and turns it to face me. It's a large print, black-and-white, of me in my messy room. The lighting is very dramatic, mostly dim except for the light my floor lamp casts on me, sitting in the corner. Around me are all of my magazine clippings tacked up on the walls, and my books and CDs and clothes are strewn across the floor. My bedspread is rumpled; the top of my chest of drawers is covered with papers and clothes. I'm staring at the camera with a look that says, *Stop looking*.

I stare harder at the face in the photograph. Is it possible that I've ever looked this intense?

"Look," Ms. Delani says, and hands me a certificate. "She won."

The certificate says, *First Prize:* Caitlin in her room, *by Ingrid Bauer.*

"I have so many photographs of you, photographs that I will never throw away. Some of them are like this one. You're very self-aware, very cognizant of being watched, but in others you aren't. She took them from across a room, or outside at a distance. You're bent over a desk, reading, or walking with your back to her, or laughing at someone else's joke. Or simply lost in thought. There are even some of you sleeping. I don't know if you realize the extent to which you inspired her. All of these photographs that she took of you . . . they fill a *drawer* in my office."

I try to grasp what she's saying. I knew that Ingrid took a lot of pictures of me, but she took a lot of pictures of everything. She always had her camera. She was always pointing it at something.

She says, "Her suicide shook me deeply. It changed so much about how I view myself, the work I do with all of you."

She sighs.

"How can I explain this?" she murmurs.

"What was it you two wrote . . ." She settles into her chair, takes her glasses off, and places them on the table. "'Picture Ms. Delani pouring spoiled milk down her drain. Picture her getting a physical. Picture her emptying her cat's litter box.'"

My throat tightens, but she smiles.

"I found one of your notes. I always wondered what you two wrote about so intently."

"I'm sorry," I say. "It was this stupid thing we did. You just always seemed so perfect."

She shakes her head. "But here's the truth: I do *all* of that. Every single thing on that list, I do. I don't know how many lists you made, or everything you wrote, but I imagine that everything you thought of, I do."

"I'm not so sure about that," I say. "We thought of a lot of things."

"Well, maybe not everything, but I am not perfect. Ingrid's death should make that absolutely clear. Apart from her parents, I was the adult that she was closest to. I was so blinded by her talent that I didn't recognize the tremendous pain behind her work. She gave me hundreds of images, so many chances to see that she was in trouble. I failed her."

I want to tell her that she failed me, too. I'm thinking about the first day of school—I was sure that she would make things better, that she would treat me as she used to.

I say, "I needed you, too." My face burns.

"Yes," she says. "I know. I'm so sorry."

I can't say anything else, and for a little while, neither can she.

Finally, she goes on. "I knew that if you reached out to me, that I would have a responsibility to you. That's why I didn't want you to be in my class at first. It isn't fair, but the image of you is so intertwined with my memories of her. When I heard of Ingrid's death, I pored over her photographs, and images of you were what I was seeing."

She pauses, waits for me to say something, but this is too much to take in, and all I can do is stare at the photograph in front of me and think that I never looked this closely at myself before, at my whole self just sitting in my room.

"You had no idea how complex a subject you were," she says. "She took photographs of you that evoke confusion, love, anger, joy . . . the full range of human emotion."

She holds another photograph out to me. I take it.

"This is one of my favorites," she says.

Raindrops. Patches of light through clouds. Me, on a swing, in the sky, smiling. Smiling. I never knew she developed it.

And then my eyes tear over. I'm swinging. It's the first time I ever ditched school, and I'm moving through the sky as the clouds break. I hear the wind. I hear myself laughing.

Ingrid, I yell. *This is the first law I've ever broken!*

Her voice: *How does it feel?*

The rain falling. The cold waking me up.

It feels perfect!

There is commotion outside the classroom. People are going to start coming in for first period, but I'm not ready for them yet. I pry my eyes from the frame in front of me. They land on the picture of me grimacing and I look away. I focus on myself swinging. That smile.

I hold it carefully, this artifact of myself. I need a few more minutes to let all of this sink in.

Ms. Delani rests her hand on my shoulder. "They bring her back a little bit," she says. "I wish they could bring her back completely."

I want to squeeze my eyes shut but I can't, not with the door opening.

Before everyone streams in, she says, "They bring *you* back a little bit, too."

Ms. Delani lets me spend first period in her back office by myself, looking through her heavy art books for inspiration. I have a lot of catching up to do if I want to pass her class. I hear her lecturing in the classroom, then the sounds of people talking, and I'm thankful to be back here, away from it all. I don't think about anything—I just turn pages, look at images, try to get myself calm.

18

Mom is home early from work. I'm lying on my bed doing math when she knocks and peeks her head around my door.

"Hi, sweetie," she says. "I'm on my way to run a few errands. Want to come?"

I sit up in bed and stretch. "What errands?"

"Dry cleaner, hardware store, Safeway. You could pick out some snacks for your lunches . . ."

I need a bunch of stuff for my treehouse: more bolts, sandpaper, clamps. "Yeah, okay," I say.

When we get to the hardware store, my mom heads to the gardening section.

I grab a basket and fill it up with the stuff I need. After I've found a few things, I remember the sixth-brace problem. I head to the rope aisle. The selection is overwhelming; there is thin rope, thick rope, rope made of metal, rope made of cloth.

I'm standing and staring at it when a guy in the hardware store's khaki uniform passes me and stops.

"Do you need some help?"

"I don't know which kind of rope to get."

"What thickness do you want?"

"It has to be pretty thick, I guess. I need it to support a person."

"How heavy of a person?"

"It needs to be able to support me."

He scans the choices. "This should be good," he says, picking up a spool of medium-width, yellow rope.

"Should I cut it myself?" I ask him, but he doesn't answer.

He's looking at something behind me. I turn to find my mom standing two feet away, her hand over her mouth, the blood draining from her face.

"What?" I ask.

The guy who was helping me backs away nervously.

"What?" I ask again.

Then I follow her gaze to my hands, to the rope. And it flashes back to me—the morning I found out about Ingrid. Before they told me how she did it, I thought about all the tools she could have used to die. The gun her dad kept in his safe, the knives in the kitchen, the pills in her mother's medicine cabinet. A rope.

"Mom," I say. "You don't think I . . ."

Her hands are shaking.

"Mom, it's not what you're thinking."

"You've been so angry." Her voice wavers. "You wouldn't meet with the therapist. You never tell us about how you're doing. I try to talk to you but you keep pushing me away. I worry about you *all the time*."

"Mom," I say. "I would never do that."

And then, in a narrow aisle of a hardware store, with millions of nails and bolts and hooks and hoses and spools of fishing wire and tiny lightbulbs and ropes and flower seeds, I step forward, I reach out, and I hug my mother for the first time in months. Her hands grab onto the back of my shirt and I can feel her chest heaving as she tries not to cry. She feels so small all of a sudden, so fragile. Without even thinking, I whisper, "I'm okay, I'm fine, I'm okay, I'm fine," over and over until she starts breathing normally again, until she lets go and steps back, cups her hand under my chin, and says, "Promise me."

"I'm okay," I say. "I promise."

19

When we get home, I find my dad in his office and lead him and my mom outside. We walk past my sad little car, through their vegetable garden, over the hill, around a few smaller trees, and up to my oak. It looks beautiful in the sunlight.

"This is what I've been working on," I say.

The ladder I built up the trunk looks straight and secure; the beams I've been able to attach extend six feet from the tree trunk, supported by sturdy braces.

"There will be one more beam there," I say. "And then I'll be able to lay all the floorboards down. I just haven't been able to build it yet." I turn to my mom. "That's what I need the rope for," I say, softer.

My mother squeezes my hand.

My dad sucks in a breath of appreciation. "A treehouse! Fantastic. I always wanted a treehouse when I was a kid."

"They aren't just for kids, though. I found this book." I open my metal toolbox, pull out the treehouse book, and hand it to them. "See?"

With Mom looking on, Dad thumbs through pages of elaborate treehouses with kitchens that have ovens and tables and pots and pans; bathrooms with claw-foot tubs and pedestal sinks; living rooms with wood-burning stoves and couches and rugs.

He stops on a page with a simpler treehouse. It's pretty big and rustic and it doesn't have electricity or anything. It was built by two brothers who just like to sit up there some days and look out over a river. "Yours is like this one, but also your own design. I like how you're building yours with the trunk going through the middle."

"I just thought that might be cool."

"It's beautiful," my mom croons.

"Stunning," says my dad.

They look so proud. I wish I could photograph their faces.

spring

1

The mornings are getting warmer. My parents' flowers are slowly blooming and their vegetables are sprouting up. I walk past the neat rows of plants and over the hill and down to my oak tree. Hoisting myself onto the branches, I think of how I will talk to Taylor soon. I can't hide from him forever. I don't want to.

I climb higher and settle myself into the rope swing my parents helped me secure to a thick branch. Yesterday, after I saw Dylan, I hauled all the leftover planks onto the part of the floor that I'd built already, so now it's easy for me to get to work sawing and hammering without making a million trips up and down.

I work for three hours, not even thinking about anything, losing myself in the sounds of the morning: the birds and the wind through the leaves and my hammer making contact with wood and metal. I finish the whole floor. I get up and step gingerly at first, to test how secure it is. After I'm convinced that it's strong

enough to hold me, I walk from one side to the other and back—
it's just as big as I wanted, twelve feet all the way across.

I stomp. I jump.

The planks are solid beneath me.

2

Before first period, from across the quad, I spot Taylor, Jayson, and
Henry walking toward me. I get a tingly feeling all over, half excited, half nervous.

Taylor and Jayson both smile at me and say hi.

"Hey," I say to Taylor. I smile at Jayson, too, and look at Henry,
thinking maybe now that I've been to his house he might acknowl-
edge my existence, but he's scowling at the ground.

"Hold on a sec," Taylor says to Jayson and Henry, and he steps
up closer to me and guides me a few steps away.

"So," he says. "I was wondering if you wanted to do something
Friday?"

"Actually," I say, "I was going to ask you the same question."

From behind Taylor, Henry says, annoyed, "Taylor, we have to go."

Taylor turns to him. "Just one second," he says, and then, to me,
"Did you have something in mind?"

"Yeah. You know Dylan? Her—"

"Okay, fine," Henry calls out. "I'm leaving, you can catch up."

"I'm coming, just a sec." Taylor rolls his eyes at me. "Clearly, I
gotta go, but yes. Whatever you want to do. I'll see you fourth period. You can tell me the specifics."

3

I don't know what to wear to the play, so I show up at Dylan's house
with a sackful of options. I lay them out on Dylan's bed and she
stands with her hip jutting out, her hand on her chin, deciding.

"It's a school play, so it shouldn't be that dressy. But it *is* in the city, and also it's opening night, so it isn't totally casual, either. Plus it's a date," she says. "Right?"

"Kind of," I say. "At least I think so."

She nods. "I think so, too."

She's wearing black as usual, but a more dressed-up version. Her pants are tight and kind of shiny and her tank top scoops down in the front and in the back, revealing her shoulder blades and the back of her neck as she leans over to examine the pattern on one of the shirt options I brought.

"This skirt," she says. "And that sweater." She pivots toward her closet. "And I have a belt for you."

I grab the clothes she chose and head into the bathroom.

"Oh," she says. "And the orange scarf. The orange scarf is adorable."

"Okay," I say, and shut the door.

Inside the bathroom, I look into Dylan's mirror. I want to look the opposite of adorable. I want to walk up Eighteenth Street to-night and look like I belong walking next to Dylan, like I know my way around the city the way she does. But then I think of me in the photograph that Ingrid took, the one that won the prize. Ms. Delani was right: I did look interesting. And I was just sitting in my room, looking like myself.

I slip off my pants and step into the green skirt that Dylan chose. It doesn't fit me the way it used to. It hangs a little. I guess I've been substituting Popsicles for too many meals lately. I take off my shirt, pull on a dark brown sweater that I took from my mom's closet. It's made out of this really soft, thin fabric. The faint out-line of my bra shows through it. Last, I buckle Dylan's wide, tan belt over the skirt. It's covered with little bronze studs and makes the whole outfit work, makes it just the slightest bit tough like I wanted it.

"You look great," Dylan says when I come out of the bathroom.

I feel her eyes scanning my body, wonder if I can really pull this sweater off.

"Really great," she says.

"Thanks," I mumble, and don't make eye contact. "But I really don't. Look at the way this skirt bunches."

"Fine," Dylan says. "Be difficult. All I'm saying is Taylor's gonna think you look gorgeous when he gets here."

Taylor shows up five minutes early, and we climb into his yellow Datsun and head onto the main road. Before we get on the freeway, we have to stop so Dylan can get a coffee, and then after we're over the bridge and finally find parking in the Mission, we go into the Dolores Park Café to get another one. This time Taylor and I order, too, and he insists on paying for all three of us.

"What a gentleman," Dylan says, grinning at him.

He turns to me. "Caitlin, did you hear that? She thinks I'm a gentleman."

The barista calls Taylor's name. I grab my coffee and go over to the bar to add sugar, hoping that if it's sweet enough, it won't be as bitter as it was when I had a macchiato with Dylan and Maddy.

"Caitlin?" It's a guy's voice, but it isn't Taylor's. I turn around to look.

Davey and Amanda are filling their coffees up right beside me. Davey's grown an Abe Lincoln beard, the kind with no mustache. Amanda's cut her hair short. Instantly, I feel a little dizzy. My head buzzes.

"Oh my God," Amanda gasps. "*Caitlin.*"

She takes a small step toward me but stops there. They used to hug me every time we saw one another, so now the space between us feels a million times longer than it actually is.

"Hi," I manage.

They seem just as startled as I feel. Amanda looks like she's trying not to cry. Davey stands completely still, like he's in shock.

"Look at you," he finally says. "You look . . ." But he doesn't finish.

"You look grown up," Amanda says.

When Davey finally moves, he reaches out, touches my shoulder light and fast.

"I'm sorry," he says. "This is hard, isn't it? But, shit, it's so good to see you. Are those your friends?" He gestures out the window, to where Dylan and Taylor are leaning against a pole, talking.

I don't know what to say. How can I say yes without making it seem like I've completely moved on from Ingrid? But there's no other way I can answer.

"Yeah."

Neither of them looks mad.

"What are you here for?" Amanda asks.

"We're going to a play."

"You should come see us sometime."

"Okay," I say, wondering if I will.

"That would be great," Davey says, and he seems so eager.

"Yeah, it would," I say. "I will."

I'm not sure how to end this conversation, and they don't seem to know how to, either. I take a step backward, toward the door.

"I still listen to that tape you made me. Like *all the time*."

"You do?" Davey asks.

"Yeah."

I look at Amanda. "And I listen to the Cure CD practically every night."

She smiles.

"Okay," I say. "Well, my friends are waiting, so I should probably . . ."

They both nod, their heads moving at the exact same time.

"Have fun," Davey says, and I walk out to the sidewalk.

4

Dylan explains that the theater department at Dolores High is really well known throughout the city. It got a grant a few years ago from a rich retired actress in Pacific Heights and they used the money to build a brand-new theater where the old gym used to be. It's obvious when I walk in that this isn't your typical high school play. It's swarming with people, all dressed nicely. A woman at the door is handing out programs. I open mine and find a picture of Maddy, looking serious and graceful, staring intently into the camera.

I show Taylor.

Dylan beams.

"She's really cute," Taylor says to her.

Dylan looks like she would like to smile wider, but it wouldn't be possible.

"I know," she says, practically crooning.

We find three seats next to one another in the third row. I sit between Dylan and Taylor. When most of the seats are taken, I see Dylan's group of friends walk in, the kids we hung out with in the park that afternoon.

"Hey, look," I say to her. She sees them and waves, but she doesn't get up. She stays sitting here with Taylor and me, and that makes me really happy, and I can hardly stand how right this feels, sitting here between them, waiting for the lights to dim and the curtain to rise.

I return to the program and see I also recognize the actor playing Romeo.

"Hey," I say to Dylan, pointing at the head shot. "This is your friend, right? The one who liked the waitress?"

"Yeah," Dylan says. "He's really good, too."

Then someone chimes a bell, and the audience goes quiet, and the room turns black. There is the rustle of the curtain rising, and then a light shines on three people onstage.

They open their mouths and speak in unison: "Two households, both alike in dignity in fair Verona where we lay our scene . . ."

I settle back in my chair.

The Capulet and Montague men fight on the stage with real swords that crash when they make contact. Dylan's friend enters.

"Is the day so young?" he asks Benvolio. He says, "Ay me, sad hours seem long." He is Romeo, and he is heartbroken. Every word is wistful. When he says, "O, teach me how I should forget to think!" I, for the first time in my life, see what the big deal is about Shakespeare.

It seems like forever before Maddy comes onstage. I can tell that Dylan's getting impatient, but I'm content listening to Romeo talk about his sadness, even if it is just over some girl who doesn't love him back. But then the scene changes, and the nurse and Capulet's wife are asking for Juliet, and Maddy walks onstage, all confidence, in a long white dress with a gold sash, and asks, "How now, who calls?"

Dylan reaches over and squeezes my wrist, and points her head at Taylor like I need to let him know *right now* that this is Maddy, the one and only amazingly beautiful and talented Maddy, onstage right in front of us. So I do. I lean over to Taylor's ear, and he tilts his face closer to mine, and I whisper, "That's Maddy."

He leans closer to me then, and when he says, "Yeah, I saw her picture, remember?" his lip grazes my earlobe and my body fills with light.

Romeo and Juliet meet; they fall in love. That girl Romeo was heartbroken over vanishes from his mind. All the actors are so good. They know all their lines, they really seem to feel everything. Juliet drinks the poison. We know she's faking it, but her nurse doesn't. She cries, "She's dead, deceased. She's dead, alack the day!" And Juliet's mother doesn't know it, either. She echoes the nurse, her voice loud and shrill, "Alack the day, she's dead, she's dead, she's dead!"

"Are you okay?" Dylan whispers to me. I look down and see my hands shaking.

I put them in my lap. I nod. Yes. I am okay.

When the real suicides come, I remind myself that these are actors. I gaze up at the stage lights as Romeo looks down at Juliet's body. When he declares, "Here, here will I remain, with worms that are my chamber-maids. O, here will I set up my everlasting rest," I think, *This is just a boy who was in love with a waitress at an all-night diner on Church Street.* "Eyes, look your last. Arms, take your last embrace! and lips, O you the doors of breath, seal with a righteous kiss a dateless bargain to engrossing death!" I try not to think of Ingrid. I try not to see her arms drip blood into her bathwater, see her body stretched out in her bathtub, letting in death. Romeo drinks the poison and I try to picture him without his costume, sitting in a diner booth, wearing a T-shirt and jeans.

When Juliet wakes to find Romeo dead, Maddy's voice is so full of feeling that it's all I can do to not listen to the words. And I realize that even though I know what's coming, I don't want to see it. I don't want to see a girl thrust a knife, even a fake knife, into her own body. I look over to Dylan, hoping for something. Her gaze is fixed on the stage, fixed on Maddy. She is riveted.

Taylor reaches down and squeezes my hand. I start filling my mind with words, any words; I try to remember the old biology facts but I can't hear them, something about dominant genes? Blue eyes and brown eyes? And as I'm trying to remember, Taylor leans over and whispers, "Turn around. Look at everyone." So I do. Mothers are dabbing their eyes with tissues; fathers are blinking hard. The girls our age are wiping their cheeks with the sleeves of their sweaters and the guys are shifting in their chairs uncomfortably.

And Taylor whispers, "I think this is a sign of a good performance," whispers, "Do you ever go to that Shakespeare festival in Orinda? It's outside, and whenever my mom takes me I'm always freezing my ass off by the end," whispers, "I saw a version of *Henry the Fifth* that they made into a western. Henry, the king, wore a cowboy hat," whispers, "Caitlin. You can look now," whispers, "It's over."

After the play we wait in the theater as most people leave.

"Caitlin," Maddy calls, coming toward me. We hug, and when we step apart she says, "I'm so glad that you came! Thank you so much for coming."

"You were amazing," I say. "I never really liked Shakespeare before tonight."

Taylor shakes her hand and says, "You should have seen all the people crying. You were really good."

We all walk outside, and Maddy and Dylan are greeted by more people, and Taylor and I just stand off to the side and wait for them. Then the crowd dies down, the rest of their friends leave, and Dylan and Maddy start kissing. A couple of random men walk by and stare at them. Taylor stares at them. *I* stare at them.

Taylor looks at me and raises an eyebrow.

"Um," I try. "They don't get to see each other that much."

"No, it's cool," Taylor says. "They seem really into each other. I like your friends."

"I like your friends, too," I say. Then, to clarify, I say, "Well, at least I like Jayson."

Taylor laughs. "Yeah, Jayson's like a brother to me. He's like my best friend in the world."

It's starting to get really cold. I pull the sleeves of my mom's sweater down over my hands. I glance over at Dylan and Maddy. They're still making out.

Taylor and I stand and look at each other awkwardly. I hear Maddy and Dylan murmuring. Then Taylor and I, at the same exact moment, step into each other, and kiss.

5

Taylor brings the map. I bring the notecards and the speakers for my iPod. Mr. James asks for volunteers to go first and Taylor and I both shoot up our hands. We hate public speaking; we want to get this out of the way.

"Taylor, Caitlin. I'm glad to see you're so eager." He takes a seat in the front row, like one of us, and looks genuinely excited.

Taylor and I shuffle up to the front. I try to ignore the cheerleaders glaring at me.

It's been a little over a week since Taylor and I kissed at the play. Since then, we've talked on the phone six times, hung out—with Dylan and Jayson, of course—during three lunches. Kissed once before first period in the parking lot, three times in the hallway after precalc, and every day after school. On Tuesday during break, Bethany, Henry's ex, was talking to Taylor as he waited for me near the English hall, and when I walked up, he said, *Bethany do you know Caitlin?* Bethany hardly glanced at me and shook her head. *Well then,* Taylor said, *meet my girlfriend, Caitlin.* And he touched my arm, right below the elbow, and Bethany said hi, but I hardly noticed.

Now I plug the speakers into the socket below the chalkboard and attach my iPod to them. I turn to a song by a French singer, Edith Piaf. My mom is obsessed with her. The recording sounds all scratchy and old, which is perfect. It isn't nearly as old as Jacques DeSoir, but it sets the mood.

Taylor and I hang our huge map of Europe up in front of the chalkboard.

He looks at me for the cue to begin. I nod. He clears his throat and looks down at his notecard.

"Jacques DeSoir," he begins, "was many things: a mathematician, a citizen of France, a lover of snails, and a pirate."

The class laughs a little. In a good way. I look down at my notes and say, "Born in the port town of Nice, he was always fascinated by water. In fact, he began his first mathematical pursuits by timing the seconds that passed between each wave on the beach that was close to his house. He got so obsessed that his mom had to come get him by the water after dark all the time, and the people of Nice nicknamed him *garçon de l'océan,* which, translated, means, 'boy of the ocean.'"

I glance at the class and everyone actually looks pretty interested. Mr. James gives me a grin and a thumbs-up.

Taylor says, "We have this map of Europe, and all the tacks here represent the places that Jacques DeSoir went on his travels. His travels began innocently. He would just work on the boats that people sailed, mostly cargo boats, and do his crazy experiments at night."

"But then," I say, "he fell in with the wrong crowd."

Everyone laughs.

We go on, with Edith Piaf singing French songs in the background, and Taylor and I telling little stories about Jacques DeSoir as we get to each tack on the map. We don't talk too much about actual math, but Mr. James seems okay with that. After about fifteen minutes, we end and people clap, and I turn off my iPod, and Taylor takes the map down. We go back to our seats. Then other people start going up, and most of them just have these hurried-looking poster boards. A couple people have sloppy PowerPoint presentations. It takes them longer to get their computers set up than it does to go through all of their boring details about their mathematicians' lives. By the time everyone else is finished, I realize that no one spent nearly as much time on their presentations as we did. Actually, I've never spent as much time as we did for any other assignment for school.

After class, Taylor says, "So do you want to hang out later?"

And even though the idea of just hanging around with Taylor sounds really good, I say, "Actually, there's something I need to do."

6

The DMV is a squat, plain building, but to me it looks like a shiny brochure of some distant tropical place, like it's saying, *Just peek inside and see all the good times you've been missing.*

I made an appointment for a driving test a few weeks ago. I didn't know if I would show up, but here I am, walking through the glass double doors, passing the security guard and all the people lined up who didn't make appointments. The driving instructor's name is Bertha and her hair is an orangey-pinky-red—a color that definitely does not exist in nature. She hardly glances at me from over her clipboard, just says my name and starts checking little boxes. She leads me out a back door to a little car and gestures for me to get in the driver's seat. I settle in as she slams the door to her side.

Just then I realize: I probably should have practiced.

Besides driving with Taylor that one day, I haven't driven for months, and back when I did, it wasn't very often. My dad took me out to the Safeway parking lot early in the mornings on a few weekends, and my mom took me on the freeway one time and said, "You're doing great!" But for the whole ten minutes I was on it, trying to go exactly sixty-five, she was holding on to her seat cushion like it was a life raft. And then there was Sal, my driver's-ed teacher. He was what you might call an underachiever. He took me out one morning and we drove around Los Cerros, and once he saw that I stayed within my lane for the most part, and used my turn signal and all that, he said, "Looks like you can drive, dear. Why don't I just sign off here that we've done our fifteen hours and we'll call it a day."

So I guess it's understandable that I feel a little nervous sitting here with Bertha, as I try to remember how a three-point turn works, and when it's okay to turn at a red light, and probably most importantly, which pedal is the gas and which is the brake.

"We'll just drive up along here," Bertha says, gesturing with her clipboard toward a perfectly empty, straight street. "Then we'll hang a right, you'll do a three-pointer for me, and we'll head back along this way."

"Okay," I say, but I don't move. I'm wondering: *gas or brake? gas or brake?* I try to remember what my dad taught me in the parking lot. I can remember that most of the mornings were clear and warm, and that he was wearing his tennis jacket, and afterward we got hot chocolate from 7-Eleven, but I can't remember which side the brake is on.

"You can start the car now," Bertha tells me.

"Oh, right," I say.

I look down at my feet and remember how my dad told me it was hard to *describe* all the things you do when you drive, that once you start doing it, your body just does it for you and you don't think about it anymore. I hear Bertha shift in her seat and get the feeling that she's about to say something, and I decide just to do it. I put my foot down on the left pedal and hope that it's the brake. I remind myself of how smooth it went with Taylor that day, how I hardly had to think about it at all. I turn the keys in the ignition and miraculously, the engine comes on and the car doesn't move. I shift into drive, press the right pedal and off we go.

I do just what Bertha says. I drive down the quiet street; I do my three-point turn, which is really so simple, almost nothing; then I drive back to the DMV's back door and park.

I turn the car off and remember to pull up the emergency brake.

Bertha checks more boxes on her clipboard and makes a few comments. Then she turns to me and says, "Congratulations."

She tells me to follow her back inside, and as we walk through the building I am filled with love for the DMV with its low ceilings and dirty floors and lines of impatient people, and most of all, Bertha, who risks her life daily so that people like me can be granted access to the wide-open roads.

"You know you can't drive with another minor in the car for a full year, correct?" Bertha says.

Her eye twitches. Is she winking at me? I think she is.

"Sure," I say, just to make her happy.

She hands me the paper off her clipboard and tells me to go wait in line. I wait and wait, and then I get my picture taken. I catch a glimpse of it on the screen. I think I'm blinking, but who cares? Before I leave, I get a new piece of paper, a temporary license to last me until the real one comes in the mail. I go outside and sit on the curb and call my mom for a ride home.

When she shows up, I stride over to her side of the car.

She rolls down her window.

"Hi, sweetheart," she says, looking at me quizzically.

"Close your eyes," I say.

"What?"

"Close your eyes!"

She does.

"Hold out your hands."

She opens her eyes, puts the car in park, then closes them again. She lifts her hands to the window. I set my temporary license on her palms.

"Open!" I squeal.

She stares into her hands, blinks, beams up at me.

"When did you . . ." she starts, but she doesn't finish the question, just unfastens her seat belt, opens the car door, and gets out. She stands beside the open door and gestures, grandly, from me to the driver's seat.

"Thank you," I say in a very formal tone, and take my rightful place behind the wheel.

When I get home I call Dylan, but she doesn't answer.

I hang up and call Taylor. He answers and I say, "I just got my license."

"You didn't have your license?" he asks.

"No. I told you, remember?"

"I guess I forgot. But, hey, that's great. You'll have to take me out soon."

I hear a beeping, and look down at the phone and see it's Dylan.

"I gotta go now," I tell Taylor. "Just wanted to tell you."

"So you'll take me out soon?"

"Maybe," I say. Then, "Yes."

I click over to Dylan. "I know you think that cars are the downfall of humanity, but I got my license today."

"That's awesome! Congrats. You want to drive me to school tomorrow?"

"Yeah." But then I get nervous. "But my car's a stick. And I've hardly driven it. I passed the test on an automatic."

Dylan says, "I can drive a stick. I'll walk to your house in the morning so we can drive together. That way, if you keep stalling in an intersection, I can take over."

"Wait," I say. "*You* can drive a stick?"

"Well, yeah," she says, like it's obvious.

"But you don't have your license."

"Yeah, I have it."

"But I thought cars were the downfall of humanity!"

"They are. But it isn't practical not to have a license. Sometimes you need one, you know? So I'll be at your house by like seven-fifteen, okay?"

7

Dylan shows up at my front door at seven, holding a thermos in each hand.

"Here," she mumbles, thrusting one toward me from the other side of the door. "Needs milk and sugar."

"Good morning," I say.

She squints and takes a sip. Black coffee drips on her chin and she wipes it off with the sleeve of her hoodie. She walks inside.

My parents are standing in the kitchen, and I see them get all excited when Dylan walks in behind me. They haven't gotten to talk to her very much and are still getting over the thrilling news that their moody daughter actually has a friend.

Dylan manages to raise one ringed-and-leather-braceleted hand in greeting. I open the fridge and grab the half-and-half. When I turn back around, we've formed a little circle of four, all looking in at one another. My parents are smiling at Dylan and she's looking back at them, sort of puzzled. She manages a weak smile. I turn around again and take the sugar jar down from the cupboard.

"So how was the play?" my mom asks.

"Play?" Dylan asks, scrunching her forehead. "Oh, the play." She leans against our kitchen counter and takes a sip of coffee. "So good," she finally says.

"Which one was it?" my dad asks.

"*Romeo and Juliet,* right?" my mom says.

I dump a spoonful of sugar into my coffee.

"Yeah. It was at my old school."

I take another spoonful.

"And you had friends in the production?"

"Her girlfriend," I say, stirring.

"Wonderful," my dad says. "I always imagined that I would enjoy acting."

They stare at her for a little longer, and Dylan and I stare at them.

"Toast?" my mom asks.

"Sure," Dylan says.

Dylan and I finish our toast and escape from my pleasant-but-awkward parents. Then it's out through the back door, over the brick patio, past my parents' tomato vines, and down to the driveway.

"Hello, little car," I say. "Ready for an adventure?"

Dylan squints. "When's the last time anyone drove it?"

"I don't know. But I start it a lot, so the battery should be fine."

I unlock my side, climb into the seat, then lean over and pull up the passenger-side lock. Dylan slides in and fastens her seat belt. As I put the key in the ignition, she picks at all the fur I ripped off the seat covers and stuffs it, piece by piece, into a pocket in her backpack.

"You have to treat your car nice," she says. "What is all this?"

I choose not to answer, just roll my eyes.

"Hey," she says, and points at my seat belt. "Buckle up, okay?"

"Yes, ma'am."

I turn the ignition and the car sputters to life. The tape player blasts at full volume, but Dylan doesn't even flinch. I put my foot on the clutch, the other on the gas, and we careen out of the driveway and onto the street. Dylan squeezes her fist shut.

"Okay, good, we're moving, now slow the fuck down a little, okay?" she yells over the music.

I laugh, just happy that I'm taking us somewhere. I slow for a red light and turn the volume down.

When the light changes to green, I take my foot off the clutch too fast and stall.

"Shit!" I turn the key in the ignition and someone in the long line of cars behind me honks.

Dylan says, "It's okay, it's no problem. They can go around you if they want."

"Shit shit shit." I turn the ignition again and mess up again and my car lurches then dies.

"Fuck!"

"You just did it a minute ago. You can do it again." She puts her hand on my shoulder. "Breathe," she commands.

I do. I try one more time to start the car. I take my foot off the break and put it onto the gas. Slowly, I ease off the clutch while pushing down on the gas pedal and the car coughs, lurches, then accelerates smoothly. I squeal, and Dylan leans back in her seat, finally relaxed.

8

We're broken up into groups in Mr. Robertson's class, brainstorming about hypocrisy in *The Scarlet Letter*, when my pencil lead breaks and I have to get up to sharpen it.

"Who uses pencils like that anymore, anyway?" Dylan teases, and looks back at the book.

I slide past her chair and make my way down the cramped aisle of desks, nearing Henry Lucas and Alicia's friends on my way to the sharpener. The girls are flirting with him as always. SPOILED traces his ear with her finger, ANGEL tugs at his fingertips. I trip over someone's backpack and hear Dylan crack up behind me. "Sorry!" I chirp, and keep moving. ANGEL's fingers are climbing up Henry's arm now. He looks annoyed.

"I'm gonna bring my new boyfriend to your party Friday, okay?" asks SPOILED. "He's older. He could supply the beverages."

For a few seconds, the sharpener drowns them out. As I pass their desks again, Henry's asking, "Who even said I'm having a party Friday?"

I slide into my seat next to Dylan.

"Do you like going to parties?" I ask her.

"Shh!" she says. "I'm counting how many times Hawthorne uses the word *ignominy* in this chapter."

"Nerd."

"I'm thinking of charting it out chapter by chapter to measure the levels of humiliation and disgrace."

"You can't turn this book into a mathematical equation," I say.

"I can try," she says from behind the open pages.

"So, anyway," I say. "Parties. What do you think about them?"

"They're fine."

"Want to know a secret?"

She sets the book down. "Sure."

"I've never been to one."

She blinks. "What do you mean?"

"I mean, I've never been to a high school party."

"You've never had beer from a keg?"

"No."

"You've never sat around with a group of tanked kids and talked about who was hot?"

"No."

"You've never locked yourself in someone's parents' bedroom and made out?"

I tilt my head, like I'm trying to remember. "Never."

"Hmm," she says. She opens her notebook and scribbles some words and numbers. Then she settles back in her chair and scrutinizes me.

"Caitlin," she announces, "that is a disgrace."

9

Taylor calls me later that night. "Can you come out?" he asks, his voice so ridiculously sweet and hopeful.

"I'll try," I say. "Call you back."

I find my parents out in the garden.

"Look!" My dad beckons me. He holds a green artichoke in each hand like trophies. "They're the first artichokes of the season."

"What do you think?" my mom asks. "Should we grill it? Maybe just with a little olive oil and salt so we can really taste the flavor . . ."

I shift from one foot to the other. I don't want to hurt their feelings, but I don't want to call Taylor back with bad news, either.

"You're cooking them tonight?" I ask.

"Why wait?" says my dad.

"Well, I was kinda wondering if I could have dinner with Taylor tonight . . ." I let this thought trail off, and check my parents' reactions. Disappointment flashes across my dad's face. My mom smiles wider, which I know is her way of masking what she really feels.

"But," I say. "I would hate to miss out on the *first artichokes of the season."*

My dad nods. "It would be a shame."

"And besides, I'm pretty sure that Taylor likes artichokes."

My parents turn gleeful—both Dylan *and* Taylor on the same day? They are in troubled-teen-parent heaven.

"Dinner will be on the table at eight-fifteen," my mom says, all principal now. "Richard, trim some basil, will you? I just need to get out of these clothes."

Back upstairs, I call Taylor.

"So," I say when he answers. "How do you feel about artichokes?"

"Artichokes?"

"The food."

"My parents are kind of conventional vegetable people," he says. "You know, carrots, peas, corn . . . that sort of thing. I don't think I've ever had artichokes."

"Well," I say, scrunching my face up in nervousness. "Tonight's your lucky night. Artichokes at my house."

I hold my breath, wait to hear how he'll answer. Somehow, I know that if there's reluctance in his voice, I'll be crushed.

"They invited me?" he asks, and to my amazement, his voice sounds almost eager.

"Yeah."

"Wait, but was it like, you asked them and they said, 'Okay, we didn't really plan for it so the servings might be small but if you really want him to come then go set another place at the table'? Or was it like, 'We'd really like to get to know Taylor better and it would make us really happy to have him for dinner'?"

He says this all hurried and I'm laughing even before he's finished.

"The second one." I giggle. "Definitely."

"What time?"

"Eight."

"Okay." I hear movement, things rustling. "Shit, it's already past seven! I'll be right there." And he hangs up.

He arrives a few minutes early, freshly showered like the last time he came over, and smelling like a bottle of cologne. My dad shakes his hand. My mom gives him a light hug. I think I see her trying not to choke, but I could be imagining it.

"Hey," he says to me from four feet away. He lifts his hand in this stiff little wave.

"Hey," I say back.

I want to kiss him.

When we're ready to eat, my mom, my dad, and I all sit in different places at the table. We're so used to being three—having a fourth person throws us off. So I sit on the side where my dad usually sits, and my mom sits across from me, instead of at the end, and my dad sits next to her, and Taylor sits next to me.

For a while there's a lot of small talk, but not the really awkward kind.

"Do you play any sports?" my dad asks.

"Not really," Taylor says. "I skate a little, though."

"He means skateboarding," I add real quick, so my parents won't make fools of themselves by asking about hockey or Rollerblading or something equally embarrassing.

"We know," my mom says teasingly.

Taylor loves the artichokes, and asks about their garden, and says that he would really like to learn how to grow vegetables.

"You're welcome to join us anytime," my dad says. "We're out there most evenings and on the weekends. Just come by." He seems to have forgotten all about Taylor's less-than-perfect first impression.

Taylor says, "Really? Awesome," and it's all I can do not to reach over and touch him. He's so close. Did I mention I want to kiss him?

After we're through eating, I go to the kitchen and open the freezer.

"Serious problem," I say. "There's no dessert."

Mom and Dad exchange looks.

"Do you two want to run to the store for some ice cream?"

"Sure," I say, trying to sound casual. "What kind do you want?"

"You choose," my dad says.

As Taylor and I are leaving, my mom brushes past me. "Straight to Safeway and back home, okay?" she whispers.

My face gets hot. "Of course," I hiss.

As soon as we get in the car, my hand is on Taylor's leg. I lean toward him.

"Wait!" he says. "They might be watching!"

He pulls out slowly, responsibly, drives down the block, turns the corner, and parks.

I unbuckle and climb into his lap, he puts his hand on my face, we kiss hard like in movie scenes that usually make me uncomfortable and squirmy. I open my eyes and see the reflection of his taillights in a house's window.

"Turn off your lights," I tell him.

He turns off the lights.

His hand moves, softly, up my shirt, across my back. I kiss his neck and taste salt, kiss harder. I squeeze my legs around him.

"We should get to the store," he murmurs, then touches my hair.

The steering wheel digs into my back but I hardly feel it, and he runs his hand down my thigh, traces the groove of my knee.

"Yeah, we should," I say.

We kiss until my mouth feels swollen.

When I pivot off his lap and back into my seat, exhausted, happy, the clock says 9:55.

"What time did we leave?"

"I don't know," I say. "We should hurry."

"7-Eleven's closer."

"Yeah, let's go there."

He turns his lights back on and starts the car. I watch him as he drives. I touch a small curl above his ear, the place where his neck fades into shoulder, down to his arm that rests on my lap.

His beautiful, freckled, perfect arm.

"Taylor," I say. And I've said his name a million times, but this time it sounds different, like I'm the first person to ever say it, like he's the only person in the world with that name.

"Yeah?"

I lace my fingers through his. He parks the car. I don't answer. All I wanted to say was his name.

"What flavor?" he asks.

"Anything with caramel."

He squeezes my hand and lets go. Opens and shuts his door. Walks into the fluorescent glow of the 7-Eleven.

10

"I think it best that you focus on moving forward," Ms. Delani tells me, consulting her grade book.

It's after school and we're in her back office. Books sit neatly on shelves, tins of tea rest on a table in the corner, her motel images line the walls.

"I love these," I tell her.

She follows my gaze to her photographs. "Thank you," she says.

"They aren't anything yet. Well, yes they are. They are the *beginnings* of something."

"What do you mean by the beginning?" I've never thought of a photograph as something leading to another. I want her to explain.

"All of my work is intimately connected to the process of coming to understand myself. My last series, the one you came to see at the gallery, dealt with fragmentation and unification."

She pulls a drawer out from a tall, wide cabinet and spreads a few photographs in front of me. "These were the beginnings of that series."

Each photograph is of a different woman in a different room. I recognize Ms. Delani in our classroom, leaning against the whiteboard, which is covered in photography vocabulary and diagrams. The next photograph was taken in a small, cluttered kitchen. A girl sits at a round table next to a stack of newspapers. She looks familiar, but I can't place her.

"That's my dad's kitchen," she says.

I look closer at the girl. She's wearing a roomy university sweatshirt and her hair is in a high ponytail. She's sprawled across the table, leaning on an elbow.

"It's *you*," I say.

"Yes."

"When you were in college?"

"No. Two years ago. You already knew me then."

"Are you serious?"

I can't hide my amazement and she laughs. I've never heard her laugh like this. She sounds younger, like someone who might be seated at the table next to me at a restaurant, or in the row behind me at the movies. Like someone Davey and Amanda would be friends with. I move on to the next photograph. Again, I hardly recognize her. Her hair is down, lying perfectly straight, skimming the tops of her shoulders. She is sitting on her knees on a bed staring straight at the camera. On either side, candles burn on bedside tables. She's wearing a tiny satin camisole. My first instinct is to be embarrassed that I'm looking at my photo teacher barely dressed, but then I remember the countless images of nudes I've seen over the last three years of her class and it seems less strange.

"I was inspired by Cindy Sherman," Ms. Delani says. "You remember learning about her work, don't you?"

I nod. "She photographs herself as different characters."

"Right, only I wasn't trying to become someone other than myself, I was working to reconcile the different parts of me: the teacher, the artist, the lover, the daughter, the friend. And so on."

"These are amazing," I say.

"They were a starting point. Much like these motel shots. The self-portraits were too literal. I moved on to household objects, but they were too static. I ended up with dolls. Still objects, but inherently representational of the female figure. By taking them apart, examining pieces separate from the rest, putting them back together, I was able to really wrestle with the issues I was working through."

"What issues are you working through now?"

She gathers her photographs and puts them back into the file drawer. I worry that what I asked was too personal.

She sighs. "Well, Caitlin, I imagine that they are issues we share. A pervasive feeling that something is missing. Darkness. Vacancy." Her photographs echo her from their spots on the wall. A dozen "Vacancy" signs glowing in the dark.

"I *always* begin too literally," she says. "But as I was saying, it's only the beginning of this project."

She turns from her pictures to me.

"So, let's get back to *you* now. What will you photograph to make up for a year's worth of shoddy pictures and missing assignments?" Her words are harsh, but she smiles as she says them.

"Aren't you going to give me an assignment?"

"I don't think so," she says. "It will be more interesting to see what you can come up with on your own."

She points to her collection of books. "If you'd like to browse these for inspiration, go ahead. I have hours' worth of grading to do."

I get up and run my fingers across their spines. Sarah Moon. Walker Evans. Mona Kuhn. All the photographers I love.

"Actually," I say, "if it's all right, I'd really like to look through the drawer you told me about. The one with all of Ingrid's pictures."

"Of course," Ms. Delani says. She points toward her cabinet. "Bottom drawer. I'll be up front. Take as much time as you need."

Ms. Delani lets me use the classroom phone to let my parents know I'll be here past dinner, and then I settle on the floor of her office and pull open the drawer. Just as she told me, there are hundreds of photographs of me. Some I recognize, others I never knew existed. I set the images of myself aside. Go on looking.

I find a photograph of Ingrid's room—paper lanterns hung at varying heights casting soft light across her magazines and scattered clothes. I set it down in front of me. I place one of her mom and dad sitting by the pool in their backyard beside it. Buried near the bottom of the file is one of her desk with colored pencils and a soda and her journal, now my journal, open to an early entry. There is one of her bathroom counter strewn with makeup and hair spray and bobby pins. Another of her reflection—a close-up of her photographing herself in the mirror. Most of her face is hidden by the camera. I touch the tip of her chin. Place it next to the others.

Ms. Delani appears in the open door. "I'm going to make myself some tea," she says. "Want a cup?"

I nod, keep searching.

Her record player. Her pink toes in brittle grass. The corner of Davey's living room: out the window, raindrops cling to telephone wires.

Ms. Delani steps around the photographs and sets a steaming mug on the windowsill next to me. She slips quietly away.

Her legs with a cut below one knee. Her dad, asleep on the sofa. I discover and sort and stare, concentrating so hard that I don't notice how dark it has become until Ms. Delani flips on the light. I blink. Stand up. Examine her office floor, covered with pieces of Ingrid's life.

I gather all the photographs I've chosen and walk out to the classroom. Ms. Delani is sipping her tea, reading a novel. I look at the clock. It's almost nine.

"Oh no," I say. "I'm sorry, I lost track of time."

She glances from her book. "No trouble," she says. "Did you find the inspiration you were looking for?"

I shake my head. "Not yet."

She shuts her novel, takes the last sip of her tea. "Sometimes inspiration strikes; other times you have to hunt it down."

"Could I borrow these?" I ask her.

She takes the group of photos from me. Looks at a couple.

"I'll get you a folder to carry them in," she says.

After I help her lock up, we walk to the parking lot together, climb into our cars, and say good night.

II

Later, after I've finished the dinner Dad reheated for me, I sit on the floor of my treehouse and lean against the one wall I've built so far. From up here I can see the faint outline of the hills, some lights from houses a mile or more away. I lie down on my back and look up at the stars. I put my headphones on and listen to some sad, wistful music. Just when it starts to get too cold, I take Ingrid's journal out of my backpack and open to the next entry. It's been so long since I've read—most of the time it's enough just to carry it with me. I turn on my flashlight and sit with my knees dangling off the edge, into the black sky.

dear jayson,

today i felt like dying. i woke up and didn't want to open my eyes. i tried to stay in one position, to force myself back into sleep. it didn't work.

When caitlin called me to see if i wanted to hang out i was snappy and mean. i told her that i had way too much to do and hung up the phone and climed back into bed with all my limbs feeling tired and heavy. but i still couldn't sleep so i got this fucked-up idea and i called these losers that caitlin and i hung out with a couple times. i made my voice all seductive over the phone. i told them, meet me at the park by the creek. and i didn't want to wimp out on my plan at the last minute so i said, and bring condoms.

and i felt nothing. i felt beyond dying, just dead.

and they were waiting for me when i got there. sitting on this rock, throwing pebbles into the dirty water. one of them looked at me and gave me this sneer. i couldn't tell if it was supposed to be nice or not. the other one kept looking at his hands.

i don't even really remember much.

i wasn't even paying that close attention.

if i ever grow up and have a kid i don't know what i'll tell her when she asks about my first time. i do know that i won't say: actually it was with two guys at once, who i didn't really know, and who weren't even that cute, and it was on a rock in a shitty public park, down by a creek with dirty water. and i won't tell her that i didn't even take my clothes off, that i just stuffed my underwear in my bag and lifted up my skirt and i won't tell her that it didn't hurt as much as i had wanted it to. that it hurt a lot, but not enough, and by the time the first guy had come and the second guy pushed into me it was just this kind of sore ache and not even real hurting. not something i would call painful.

but jayson, i wanted to tell you i'm sorry that i fucked it all up. and i know that if i ever get the chance to touch you it won't be the way it was meant to be, but i'm still hoping for it.

so we'll meet again in a few years, and that'll give me enough time to get myself all figured out and get off the medication and out of therapy. you'll be representing our country in the olympics. you'll run so fast you'll look just like a blur. and i'll be there photographing you for the new york times or something, and catch this amazing shot of you just as you cross the finish line with everyone else yards behind you. and we'll have sex that night in your five star hotel room. we'll call it making love. and you'll take all your clothes off and i'll take off all of mine. and you'll take the time to kiss me. and i'll be better so i won't want it to hurt anymore. i'll be like a normal person. when you touch me soft i'll think it feels nice. and maybe if i ever have a little girl someday this is the story i'll tell her instead of the other one. i'll tell her about the view from the hotel window and the way you touched my lips with your fingers before we kissed.

love,
ingrid

I look out at the black sky, and try to understand how Ingrid could have done this. I try to remember those guys, to picture them more clearly. I think one of their names was Kevin. Kevin and Lewis, maybe. Leroy? Kevin and Leroy? When exactly was this? What else was going on in my life on this day? I can't believe that I could have seen her after this, the day after or even that night, and not have known. But that's exactly what must have happened. Maybe she knew she could act like nothing had changed; maybe she got that good at pretending. Or maybe she thought that I would have noticed, and was disappointed when I didn't.

Through a few branches, I can see a light in my house switch off. It's my parents' bedroom, and I imagine them climbing into bed, worrying about me out here. I know I should go back inside so they'll get to sleep, but I can't do that right now, even though it sounds good to climb down and leave the cold and try to forget about everything for a little while. Instead, I keep reading. The letters are short this time, one after another.

DEAR TODAY,

i spend all of you pretending i'm ok when i'm not, pretending i'm happy when i'm not, pretending about everything to everyone.

love,
ingrid

dear mom,

i hate you.

love,
ingrid

DEAR DAD,

i'm sorry.

Love,
ingrid

DEAR JAYSON,

why don't you love me yet?

DEAR MOM,

i take it back.

I keep turning the pages until I find a longer entry. *dear caitlin,* I read, *this is a real letter.* My heart stops. I shut the book.

There was no suicide note. That's something I knew for sure. Her mom called my parents and told them—no good-bye, no suicide note.

But now. After so many months.

The night is cold. My parents must be tossing and turning or fast asleep. I open the book and flip through the rest of the pages.

They are all blank after this.

I knew it was coming, but it's still hard to understand that after I read this, there will be nothing left of her for me to discover. I turn my flashlight off and all the light that's left comes from the moon and the living room of my house. A gust of wind comes. All the leaves above and below and around me rustle. It's the sound of losing, or of starting over. I can't decide which.

I turn my flashlight on. I read.

DEAR CAITLIN,

This is a real letter. I hope you get this far but i won't
be mad if you don't want to read any of it. this is what
i want so don't be sad. you might be looking for reasons
but there are no reasons. the sun stopped shining for me
is all. the whole story is: i am sad. i am sad all the time
and the sadness is so heavy that i can't get away from it.
not ever. there used to be days that i thought i was okay,
or at least that i was going to be. we'd be hanging out
somewhere and everything would just fit right and i would
think 'it will be okay if if can just be like this forever' but
of course nothing can ever stay just how it is forever.

i don't want to hurt you or anybody so just please forget
about me. just try. find yourself a better friend. i never
laughed as hard as i laughed with you but now not even
the laughing feels good.

                        LOVE,
                        INGRID

For what feels like a million years, I lie on the hard, cold floor of my treehouse. Then, somehow, I climb down the ladder, feel my way through the dark of the yard, turn off all the lights in my house, and make it to my room.

I have her journal. I have her photographs. But still. There is so much missing. I crawl under my blankets and curl my body as tight as I can. I shiver and rub my feet together. Try so hard to get the cold out.

12

In the morning, I make my way down the stairs and find my parents in the kitchen.

"I don't think I'm up for school today," I tell them. They exchange glances. I trace the outline of the doorknob with my finger. "I want to stay home and finish my treehouse."

I look down at the kitchen floor and move my blue sock along the gray tiles. I know my parents are giving each other silent messages.

"What about your schoolwork?" my dad eventually asks.

"Could you get the assignments from Dylan?" my mom suggests. I nod.

"Okay, then," says my dad.

"But only today," adds my mom.

"Thank you," I say, and trudge back upstairs.

Later, after my parents have left, I go back down to the kitchen and make a bowl of cereal. I sit at the table, where my dad has left his newspapers in a pile. On the cover of the *San Francisco Chronicle* are pictures of war—a woman screaming; a bombed-out, faraway city. I sort through the stack for the *Los Cerros Tribune,* in search of milder news.

I find it, eat a spoonful of cornflakes, and scan the headlines:

NEW GOLF COURSE PLAN APPROVED, LOCAL DOG WINS NATIONAL COMPETITION, DATE SET FOR DEMOLITION. I cast the paper aside and pour myself a cup of coffee. I already know that I don't like regular coffee, but I think I know what is being demolished, and I need a minute to collect myself.

I take a sip and dump the rest out.

I return to the table, gather the courage, and read.

After months of debate regarding the long-closed Parkside Theater between Cherry Ave. and Magnolia Ave. on the west side of Los Cerros, the owner of the land, with a private developer, has scheduled the demolition for June 25 of this year . . .

13

At ten, I start on the treehouse. My arms and legs feel heavy and tired, but I force myself to keep moving. It takes me until two to finish the fourth wall, but the next two go faster. As I lift and pound, I try to keep my head clear, but every minute it swims with thoughts of her.

I wrote a speech for the funeral. I was too sad and out of it to write anything good, but I knew that if I had died, I would have wanted Ingrid to write a speech for me. I got up there, to the podium. I put the paper down so that I could read it, but then the letters didn't make sense. I couldn't read them in order. There were certain words that I could focus on, *friend* and *talent* and *remember,* but everything else was blurry. I don't know how long I stood up there before Davey came and took my arm. *Come on,* he said. *You don't have to do this.* And I followed him down the platform and back to my parents, because it was easier than being up there alone.

———

I'm leaving huge openings in the center of all the walls. What's the point of a treehouse if you don't have a view? I attach long, thick canvas curtains above the openings, and hooks below to tie them down in case of rain and wind.

Later that day, at the cemetery, when Ingrid's casket was about to be lowered into the ground, I covered my eyes. I thought it would be better that way, but it was worse because Ingrid's mom let out this terrible sound. It wasn't a scream and it wasn't a moan. It was something I'll never be able to describe, something that stayed in my ears for months, all during my family's escape to the forest.

When my dad gets home from work, I ask for his help. He changes into a sweatsuit and comes out to the treehouse to see what I need.

"What progress!" He claps his hands.

The clap stays in the air. Everything else is quiet. He waits for me to tell him what to do, but I stand with my arms limp at my sides.

"Honey," he says. "Honey."

He wipes tears off my face and then snot. He uses his hands. He loves me that much.

"The roof," I say.

"What?" He searches my face, trying to figure out what a roof has to do with why I'm crying.

"I need help with the roof."

He scans the yard and sees the long beams waiting. Then he walks over to the pile and lifts one. "Do you want to climb up first and I'll come after and hand it to you?"

———

At the cemetery, when I opened my eyes again, Ingrid's dad was holding on to her mom, who was making normal sobbing sounds by then, and he was completely silent, but his whole body was shaking like crazy, like he was caught in a personal earthquake.

My dad looks lost in his sweatsuit and sneakers, waiting for an answer.

"Yes," I say. "I'll go first." And I start climbing.

14

After dinner I put my pajamas on, get into bed, and just lie there. At eight, Dylan calls.

"You want the English homework?"

"I guess."

"We're supposed to read the first three chapters of *Frankenstein* and write a page-long response about the relationship between Mary Shelley's dedication to her dad and the discussion of parenting in the book."

"Okay."

"Do you want to write it down?"

"Not really."

She's quiet. "Do you want me to come over? Do you need to talk?"

"I'm just tired."

"I know it's more than that."

I stare at the photo of Ingrid on my wall. "I'm sorry," I say. I can hardly talk. My voice comes out slow and groggy. "Please don't be mad. I just can't talk right now."

I pull the covers over my head. I open my eyes under the blankets and I can barely make out the little star pattern of my sheets.

"Caitlin," she says. Her voice is soft. "You're going to have to talk about it sometime."

"I know." I nod, even though I know she can't see me.

15

The garage is a terrifying, claustrophobic mess of junk that my parents refuse to throw away, but right now, as I dig through it, I feel like a sweepstakes winner collecting on my prize. It's too good to be true that any of this stuff—the old globe where the Soviet Union still exists, the five Persian rugs from when my mom was obsessed with auctions, the countless candleholders and little figurine things that my dad's held on to from the seventies—any or all of this could be mine.

I'm furnishing my treehouse. Under boxes of dusty records, I find a rug with a blue and green design, bordered by a pretty amber color. Pushing more boxes aside on one of the shelves, I find some of my dad's old things. I read the dirty quotes in his yearbooks and find his junior-year picture. His hair is a little long around the ears and he's wearing a leather cord as a necklace. He looks surprisingly cool. Next, I find a hummingbird feeder that's made of carved wood and glass. I hold it toward the lightbulb in the ceiling to get a better look at it. Whoever made it carved bird shapes into the wood and painted their beaks yellow and their eyes blue. The tips of their wings are painted red. I put it with the rug.

Soon it gets hard to breathe. Dust is everywhere. I grab a battery-operated boom box and a couple empty wine crates and escape into the fresh air. Before shutting the garage door, I pull out an old cardboard box and rip off a little part of it. In the house, I get a marker and tape to attach it to a stick. Like a little kid I write, KEEP OUT.

Once I get everything brought up the treehouse ladder, I'm too tired to do anything else. I unroll the rug and lie down on top of it. It's a little dusty, but at this point I don't really care. I lie there and look out one of the windows across all the other trees. Up here, from this angle, it looks like I'm in the middle of a forest. I don't close my eyes; I don't fall asleep. I just stare out the opening and listen to the faraway sounds of cars on the road in front of the house.

———

Later, I hear footsteps through the yard, getting closer. I'm afraid it's my parents because I decided to stay home from school again today, and I doubt they'll be thrilled. The footsteps stop at the base of the tree. I hope my sign works.

Then I hear Dylan's voice. "Is this real?" she asks.

I don't get up because I don't want her to see me. "It's a joke," I yell down.

"So can I come up, then?"

"No."

I wait for her to say something else, but there's just quiet, followed by the sound of her stomping away.

"Wait!" I yell. Her footsteps stop. I climb down.

"Let's go somewhere else," I say.

16

At the noodle place, sitting across from Dylan at our favorite booth, I confess.

"I have her journal."

Dylan's coffee mug is lifted to her mouth, but she doesn't sip.

"She slid it under my bed before she killed herself. At least I'm pretty sure she slid it under."

She lowers her mug to the table, and fixes me with the kind of stare only she can pull off, the kind that usually makes me squirm under the pressure of it. But this time, I just stare back.

I repeat myself: "I have her journal."

She sips.

Holds the coffee in her mouth.

Swallows slowly.

Whispers, "*Fuck.*"

Murmurs, "Why haven't you told me?"

Reaches across to my arm.

She keeps her hand there until the waiter comes with our soup and surveys our table nervously, not sure where to set the giant bowls, and she has to let go. I open my backpack, and pull the journal out—black cover, a Wite-Out bird half chipped off. I hand it to her over the steam that rises from our soup. She takes it and looks down at the cover. Her hands are shaking, but her hands are always shaking. It could be the coffee, but I don't think so.

She opens to the first page. I know it so well by now. I've probably memorized every entry. She is studying Ingrid's self-portrait, reading what she wrote above it: *me on a sunday morning*. I keep wondering, *What Sunday? What was I doing when she was drawing that? Where was I when she was watching the Wite-Out dry?*

I ask, "What about you?"

She looks, confused, from the journal.

"I want to know what happened to you. I know there was something."

She looks back down, turns to the next page.

"Another time," she says.

"When?"

"Later."

"Later tonight?"

She doesn't answer me. She turns to the last entry. While she reads, I carefully tear my napkin into strips.

17

It is later. We are in my room.

Dylan sits cross-legged on my floor and sets her hands, palms up, on her lap.

"I had a brother," she says. "His name was Danny. You remember that picture in my room? The one you said was cute? That was him."

I do remember, but I just nod, don't say anything.

"When I was eleven and he was three, he got really sick."

Dylan stops. She stares into her empty hands. Stays silent until her breathing steadies. She's wearing a tank top and I can see the definition in her wiry arms. Her eyes look huge, greener than I remember.

When she talks again, her voice is so quiet I can barely hear her. "We tried," she says. "We did everything we could. At the end he was so weak."

I can't look at her anymore, so I study the carpet. I remember the picture of him on her desk, and remember asking her about it, but I can't think of the words I used. It's hard for me to accept that I didn't notice that he looked like her, or wonder why she didn't say anything about it.

"Dylan," I start. I don't know what I'm going to say next, but I know I have to say something. "That must have been—" I try, but Dylan shakes her head, cuts me off.

"After it happened, we all felt alone. I was sure there was no way my parents could understand the way I felt, and my mom thought that my dad had no clue how much it hurt her because he still went to work every day. My dad thought that my mom couldn't even begin to understand what it was like for him to lose his son. They had to split up for a year before they could understand the way they were hurting."

I'm lying on the edge of the bed, watching her. I want to take her hand like she did for me earlier. I reach out, but she pulls back, only slightly, but enough for me to know that she doesn't want to be consoled.

I sit up. "Tell me three things about him."

She looks at me, surprised, but knows exactly how to answer.

"He loved chasing pigeons. Whenever he recited the alphabet, he switched the *B* and the *D*. He'd say, 'A-D-C-B-E-F-G.'"

I smile and wait. When a minute passes, I say, "One more."

"He had the strongest little arms," Dylan says. "He used to hug me around the neck so hard it hurt."

It's getting dark fast. Dylan tips her head up to my ceiling. Her face glows blue.

"I know how you feel," she says. "Believe me. But you are not the only one hurting over Ingrid."

She sits there for a minute longer and I think she's going to say more, but she doesn't. Instead, she climbs onto my bed and hugs me, tight and awkward, her arms squeezed around mine so I can't hug back. It takes me by surprise. It knocks the wind out of me. She lets go and walks down the stairs and out the front door.

I sit still for a long time. I can still feel the pressure of her arms around me. Down the hall my parents are talking, brushing teeth, opening drawers. I unzip my backpack and take out Ingrid's journal. I lay it, exposed, on my desk. When I know my parents are asleep, I cross the room to my window. I look down at my car. Out at the sky.

An idea comes. I wait for morning.

18

Hope starts over. At 8 A.M., I'm out the sliding-glass door and onto the patio, note left for my parents next to the espresso machine explaining everything I'm about to do, bag heavy with all the things I'll need for today. I pass the last stack of wood, the planter boxes of yellow flowers, my parents' tomatoes reddening on their vines.

When I slide into my car, the fake fur of the driver's seat feels soft against my legs. I'm wearing a skirt I haven't worn for a year— green and yellow checkered, short enough to show my pale, sharp knees. I start the ignition, remembering Taylor's fingertips running down my thighs. Deep in my stomach, something tightens. In a good way.

I shift to first gear, and pull quietly out the driveway. I don't want to wake my parents on the only morning they sleep in.

Even though I love Davey's tape, I feel like listening to something new, so at all the red lights on the way to the freeway I search for good songs on the radio. Static crackles through the speakers, followed by talk radio, a sappy love song, a preacher with a voice like gravel, then a song that I love—a perfect morning song. I roll my windows down, turn the volume up, sing along loud as I roll past all the sleepy streets.

I turn left onto the on-ramp to the freeway, build up speed, then shift into fifth gear. At first, the freeway is practically empty, but as I get farther from the suburbs, more cars appear. I glance into their windows and try to guess where they're going.

Asian man in a Lexus—into the office on a Saturday? I imagine his daughter saying, *Dad, you work too hard.* I steal another glance at his face; he looks perfectly content, so I figure he enjoys his work. Old woman hunched over her steering wheel—off to breakfast with her knitting group, thinking, *Today, I'll finish the first sleeve on my husband's sweater.*

As the tollbooth approaches, I grip the steering wheel harder, and try to fend off all traces of panic. I'm about to drive over the bridge for the first time, and right now it feels a little like diving off a cliff. The guy at the tollbooth is listening to headphones and dancing. I give him a ten and he hands back my change, and from there I'm on my own. I have to merge with about a million cars on each side and I let out a yelp of sheer terror, but miraculously, I survive it. What comes next is terrifying, but might also be the most exhilarating moment of my life.

I've been on the bridge so many times, but it's never felt like this. The land drops out beneath me. On each side is water and a few boats, so distant they look like toys bobbing along the surface of the bay. Above me are thick, strong cables, holding the bridge up. Above them: sky. A gust of wind comes and I hold hard to the steering wheel to stay steady. Treasure Island approaches, and I'm driving over land again, and then Treasure Island is only a speck in my rearview mirror, and I'm back over water, the city stretching in front of me, dense with possibility.

I exit onto Duboce Street, turn left, and pull out the directions I printed this morning. I navigate down streets that are new to me. The directions have me take a different route from the one Dylan and I walked that afternoon a couple months ago, but I follow them carefully, and soon I find a parking spot and turn off the car.

I drop a few quarters in the meter and walk through the door of Copy Cat.

Maddy sees me first and calls to me from behind the counter. I grin, relieved—I hadn't known for sure that she'd be working. She finishes ringing up a customer, and I wait for her in the corner of the store because I'm not sure if she's allowed to have friends visit. I don't want to get her in trouble with her boss. But as soon as she's finished, she prances toward me in her apron and gives me a hug.

"What are you doing here?" She cocks her head in curiosity.

"I need to make some copies," I say, like it's obvious.

Maddy laughs. "There aren't any copy stores in Los Cerros?"

I reach into my bag, pull out Ingrid's journal.

"Copies of this."

Maddy takes the journal from me. I don't know if Dylan's told her about it, if it will mean anything to her. But she holds it in one hand, puts her other hand on my arm, says, "Oh, of course."

She looks pensive for a moment. "I can ask my manager if you can use the back room. We work on the big orders there and it's a lot more private."

Out here, light streams through the windows, faint music plays, a woman with tattoos covering both arms uses one copier, a gray-haired man with rings on all his fingers has papers spread out over a worktable. Between them, an unused copy machine and table wait against a wall of windows.

"Thanks," I say. "But I'm actually fine here."

"Okay," Maddy chirps. "Let's get you set up."

She guides me to a display of paper.

"Why don't you use this," she says, reaching for a stack near the top. "It's really nice quality. Here, feel it."

It's slightly textured and thicker than normal paper.

"It's kinda expensive," she whispers, "but you can use my discount."

I glance around for a manager, but all the people working seem young and nice.

"Yeah, okay," I whisper back.

At the machine, I breathe in the smell of ink and paper.

She shows me how to get the settings right, and once I've gotten the hang of it, she goes back behind the counter.

Out the window, people are strolling by, pushing strollers, walking dogs, sipping coffee. A few couples wait, relaxed, outside a restaurant. I open to Ingrid's first page and wonder how many hours I've spent staring down at it, alone, looking for answers or comfort.

I place it down on the lighted glass, close the lid, press START.

A second later, a perfect copy spits out of the machine. I pick it up and hold it. There is her crooked smile, her yellow hair.

I press start again.

19

An hour later, I'm finished. I carry my thick stack of copies to the counter and Maddy rings me up.

She reaches under the counter, pulls out a piece of thick, brown paper, and folds it around my copies. "So Dylan told you about Danny. That's huge. She *never* talks about Danny."

She pauses, but her face looks thoughtful, so I wait for her to say more.

"She doesn't let too many people get close to her. She's very guarded. But she really cares about you, and she knows how it feels to go through something like this."

She unfolds a bag and rests my copies inside.

I don't want to take it. I don't want to leave the store. Everything feels perfect—the sunshine, the music, the woman and her tattoos still working away on some never-ending project, Maddy smiling kindly from across the counter—then it hits me.

This is how it feels to have friends.

It isn't something fleeting. It won't end when I walk out the door.

I take the bag, reach in, and find a copy of a drawing Ingrid did of a girl's skirt and legs. At the bottom it says, *Brave*.

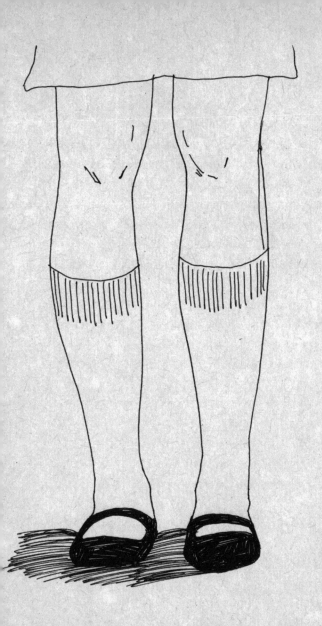

Brave

"I want you to have this."

Maddy lifts it to eye level, grasping it gently on both sides.

"Tell me about it," she asks, without looking away.

I lean over the counter so I can get a better look. "It's from the middle of her journal, where she seems really confused in most of the entries. But it seemed like she still had some hope then." I shrug. "I don't really know anything else about it."

I think of driving earlier, the man on his way to work, the old woman and her sweater. "We could make it up," I suggest.

"So, let's see," Maddy says. "She was sitting outside somewhere in your town."

"On the steps by the Starbucks."

"Waiting for you."

"My mom was gonna drop me off to meet her."

"So she was just watching people, wasting time till you got there."

"And she saw a girl."

"An eleven-year-old."

"And she thought she was cute."

"But didn't want the girl to see her staring."

"So she only sketched the bottom half of her."

"And then . . ." Maddy says. "Your mom pulled up and you hopped out of the car."

"And she shut her journal 'cause she was always really private about it."

"But later that night she opened it again, and thought the picture was missing something."

"So she thought about it," I say, and as I invent the next part of the story, I really picture Ingrid, sitting at her colored-pencil and watercolor-covered desk. "And she remembered what it was like to be an eleven-year-old girl, either scrawny and flat-chested . . ."

"Or chubby and too embarrassed to tell your mom you need a bigger training bra."

"And she thought that it was hard."

"It was really *hard* . . ."

"To be eleven, and be a girl."

"So she got out her black pen . . ." I say.

"And she wrote the word *brave*."

Maddy lowers the picture and smiles. I smile back.

"See you soon?" she asks.

"Yeah," I say. "I'll see you soon."

20

In the car, I open my notebook to the second page of directions—
from Copy Cat to Davey and Amanda's apartment in Hayes Valley.
By now, lots of people are on the road, and I creep through city traffic
for about twenty minutes before I get to their street. This time, finding parking is harder, and when I finally spot someone leaving, I have
to block the lane while I wait with my turn signal on. "I'm sorry I'm
sorry I'm sorry," I say to all the cars that swerve around me. It takes
me at least ten tries before I'm parallel-parked, and by the time I've
climbed out of the car, the traffic has quieted down a little. I walk
a couple blocks, past a café with stylish people inside, past a skinny
man smoking a cigarette, past a million Victorian apartments rising
on either side of me. A homeless guy in a worn gray sweater asks me
for a quarter, and I reach into my bag and fish out a dollar.

"God bless you," he says, walking away. A few steps later he adds,
"You're a sweetheart." When he's reached the end of the block, he
shouts, "Be good! Listen to your parents! Stay in school!"

I find their apartment—a light blue Victorian with gold trim. I
look up at the top floor, but I can't see anything through the windows. I don't ring the doorbell yet. Instead, I imagine what would
happen if everyone turned their regrets into wishes, went around
shouting them. Signal lights would change at intersections, and
as the people on opposite sides of the street stepped off the curbs,
they would call to one another—*Finish college! Exercise at least*

three times a week! Never start smoking! Tell your mother you love
her! Wear a condom! Make peace with your brother! Don't sign any-
thing before you've met with a lawyer! Take your dog to the park!
Keep in touch with your friends!

I ring Davey's doorbell and wait for footsteps down the stairs,
for the lock to turn.

Nothing.

I ring again, just in case.

After another minute, I sit on their front steps and find the pages
I want to give them—her first entry, the one to the hall monitor,
because I know it will remind them of how much energy Ingrid
used to have; a couple pages of mushy Jayson dreaming, because
I'm pretty sure that they never got to know that side of her; and
one of the last entries, even though I feel a little mean, like I'm
dropping a bomb on all the good memories. But, at the same time,
I'm doing this to share her, and that means all of her—the ener-
getic, hopeful Ingrid, the sad Ingrid, the violent Ingrid, the Ingrid
who hated me sometimes.

After I get their pages together, I tear out a sheet from my notebook and I write them a note. Then, I paper-clip everything together, and leave their package in the mailbox.

> *Dear Davey and Amanda,*
>
> *I know I said I'd stop by a while ago. I'm sorry it's taken*
> *me this long. Here is something I wanted you to have.*
> *If you're sad, make sure to talk about it!*
>
> *Love,*
> *Caitlin*

It's already noon and I'm hungry, so I go back to that café I passed
earlier, and order a sandwich and a latte and sit at a table, sur-

rounded by older people wearing black and talking about important things.

A girl in a vintage cocktail dress calls me from behind the counter, so I weave between the other tables to get my food. I look through the copies as I eat, deciding which ones I'll give to my parents. I take a sip of the latte, and decide I'll give them one of everything. I take another sip. Then another. Even after the foam is gone, the drink still tastes good, kind of milky, not too strong. And maybe I'm overreacting, but it makes me so happy—I've been searching this whole year to find a coffee drink that's right for me, and now I've found it.

21

It is 2 P.M. I'm back in Los Cerros.

A man answers the door at Jayson's house, wearing sweats and an Oakland A's T-shirt. He's tall like Jayson, but not as athletic-looking. Behind him is a small living room with a worn-in couch and a recliner. A television is playing commercials.

"Mr. Michaels?" I ask.

"That's me," he says.

"I'm Caitlin. I'm a friend of Jayson's . . ."

He opens the door wider. "Come in," he says. "Jayson and I are watching the game."

"Jay-son!" Mr. Michaels calls as I walk in.

Jayson emerges from what I imagine is the kitchen, carrying a huge bowl of popcorn and wearing a backward A's hat. I crack up.

"Big fans?" I ask them, and they laugh, nod their heads as if to say I've found them out.

I share their popcorn and Mr. Michaels has me sit in his recliner, an honor, he tells me, which is reserved for only very special guests. Jayson rolls his eyes.

By the middle of the third inning, I'm starting to get nervous. I have so much more to do today, but I can't figure out how to give Jayson his entries without making a big scene in front of his dad. I try to catch his eye, and when I finally do, I point my head toward the door. I do it subtly, *too* subtly I guess, 'cause Jayson just looks confused and asks, "You want more popcorn?"

"Okay," I say helplessly and he hands me the bowl.

Another inning passes and I'm getting desperate, so I just hope that Jayson was taught to walk his guests to the door, and tell them I have to get going.

"I'll walk you," Jayson says, and I want to hug him.

Once we're out the door, Jayson tells me, "My dad's totally gonna grill me when I get back inside, you know."

"Sorry," I say, knowing how weird it seems that I just showed up out of nowhere and watched half a game with them.

"No, it's cool," Jayson assures me. "We're friends, you can come by anytime. But my dad's gonna think you want to date me. He'll be bummed when I tell him it's not like that. Plenty of girls have come over before, but he's never offered one of them his recliner."

"Yeah, right."

"No, I'm serious. He totally likes you."

"Oh no!" I laugh. "I'm sorry to disappoint your dad. He's so nice."

Jayson waits while I unlock my car door and set my heavy bag down on the seat.

"What do you have in there?" he asks.

"Too much," I say. "But some of it's for you."

"Oh yeah?"

I pull out his pages and place them in his hands.

"They're copies I made from one of Ingrid's journals."

Jayson slides into my car and turns the light on inside. I sit up on my trunk, and give him time to look.

I've been trying to be honest about what I give people, but after thinking a lot about it, I decided to give Jayson only the good parts. I don't think that the rest is something he would want to know, and I'm pretty sure Ingrid wouldn't have wanted him to know, either.

I wait for what feels like an hour, and then I go back to where he's sitting.

He's hunched over the steering wheel with his head in his hands.

"Jayson," I say.

He doesn't move.

I feel a sudden burst of regret, like this was the worst thing I could have done.

"Jayson?"

I put my hand on his shoulder, searching for some way to make this right. I thought it would be good. I keep thinking about what he said on her birthday—*I felt like telling everyone that it was different for me, but I knew that was stupid. I didn't deserve it, I wasn't even close.* I really thought it would be good, but I realize I was wrong. This was too much for him to take. It's true—he didn't even know her that well. So they sat next to each other in bio, and once he said he liked her hat, but really, that was it. And now I've bombarded him with this.

"Jayson."

I squeeze his shoulder.

"*Jayson,*" I plead.

And he snaps out of it, lifts his head, climbs out of the car.

His face is wet. He says, "You have no idea how this makes me feel."

And I open my mouth to tell him that I'm so sorry, but he opens his first.

"Thank you."

22

The next place I drive to I know so well, almost as well as my own house. I pull onto the shady, tree-lined street, stop the car, and just sit.

It was hard to ring Davey's doorbell this morning, but this feels worse than hard—it feels impossible. I wipe my hands on my skirt and glance over at the driveway. Her mom's car is there. Her dad's is, too. I feel like I'm standing at a high altitude, where the air is thin and icy and painful to breathe.

I take my bag from the passenger's seat.

As I approach the walkway that spans their front lawn to their door, I realize that I should have given them some warning. I should have at least called an hour earlier or something to see if now was an okay time. But if I leave, I have no idea how long it will take me to get the courage to come back. I hesitate on their front stoop, force Ingrid's drawing of the girl into my head, think, *Brave.*

I knock—three quick taps followed by two slower ones—the way I used to when I'd come over all the time, and I didn't wait for anyone to open the door, just announced my presence and let myself in. Ingrid's dog starts barking at the door, and I hear Susan calming him. I brace myself for her to look completely different, promise myself I won't let her see my shock when I see that she's become a different person, a skeleton, a shell.

The door eases open.

Her hair is grayer, longer. She looks a little heavier, but mostly she looks the same.

I open my mouth, but can't think of what to say. Last time I was here, I'm sure I breezed past her, hardly noticed her, went straight to hang out with Ingrid in her room.

"Oh my." She covers her mouth with her hand, but I can see from her eyes that she's smiling.

"Hi, Susan."

She touches my shoulder.

"Come in," she says, collecting herself. "What a surprise. What a nice surprise."

I follow her to the living room, but freeze when I step inside.

In the center of the main wall, above the fireplace, hangs Ingrid's winning portrait.

Susan glances toward the photo, glances toward me. She smiles, gently. "Is it strange to see yourself above my mantel?"

"A little," I manage.

"Veena gave it to us."

I nod.

"She brought it to us the evening after she showed you."

It feels strange to hear her mention Ms. Delani, to know that Susan knows little things about me, like what day it was that I saw that photograph. All this time, I've been trying so hard to not think about Ingrid's parents, so hard that for a while it was like they didn't exist.

"You look beautiful," Susan says.

In the photo, I'm in a plain tank top and grungy jeans. My hair's messy and I look tired—whatever night Ingrid took it, I wasn't exactly looking my best.

"I mean now," Susan says. Then, "You look older."

And I know she doesn't mean it this way, but I can't help but think, *Older than Ingrid will ever look*. I feel my eyes welling up. I thought I'd given myself enough time to prepare for this. Almost a year should have been enough time.

"Mitch is taking a nap," Susan says. "He had a tough week at work. Why don't you sit down and I'll go get him. He'll be so happy to see you."

I sit on their leather couch, slip my shoes off, and curl my legs under me. I have the entries I'm giving them all picked out, but as I look through them I feel like they aren't enough. I wish I framed them or bound them in a little book.

Footsteps come from down the hall, and then Ingrid's dad is in front of me, his arms around me, lifting me up. I don't know how to react—Mitch was never like this before. He was always nice, but was never the hugging type. He doesn't say anything, just holds me tightly, desperately, and from over his shoulder, I can see Susan's mascara pool around her eyes and streak her face, and this is worse than I thought it would be, and I hate myself so much right now because I know it's awful, but I want nothing more than for him to let me go. His arms get tighter and I bite the inside of my mouth to keep myself from shouting, *I'm not her, I'm not your daughter, stop pretending I'm your daughter.* But he holds on. It hurts to breathe. I'm here, I'm in this house, and I'm seeing it the way Susan and Mitch saw it: waking in the morning to the sound of water running from the bathroom down the hall, thinking it must be Ingrid taking her shower a little early, fading back to sleep, waking up again to the sound of the alarm, Mitch asking, *Suzy, do you hear that?* Susan answering, *Yes.* Down the hall, the pat of two sets of slippers. *Mitch, wait here, I'll see if she's showering.* A tap on the bathroom door. *Ingrid?* Another tap, louder. *Ingrid!* The groan of hinges, the water, the smell—like urine, like heartbreak, like metal. *Oh my God.* Red everywhere. *Suzy, what? Suzy, I'm coming in.* Their daughter, naked—breasts and pubic hair, hips, and wounds, and blood, and skin, and half-closed, still eyes. And my legs are trembling, and Mitch's arms are like a straitjacket, and Susan cries in the doorway, and I swallow the blood in my mouth, force my voice to come out steady when I whisper, "Hey, Mitch," to remind him that it's only me.

23

I'm back on the couch, sitting kind of awkwardly with my legs tucked under me because I'm not used to wearing skirts anymore, especially short ones.

Mitch sits on the opposite couch, looking a little shell-shocked. Every now and then he glances at me and shoots a nervous smile in my direction. Susan comes back from the kitchen, carrying a pitcher of lemonade and three glasses.

She pours my glass and sets it on the coffee table. "I made this from lemons your mom and dad grew," she says. "Your mom gave me a whole bagful last week."

"I didn't know you saw my mom last week," I say, surprised.

As Susan pours glasses for herself and Mitch, she tells me that she has lunch with my mom almost every week, and again it feels strange that so much could be going on without me even knowing.

When my lemonade is half gone, and our conversation subsides for a moment, I pull out the pages I chose for them.

I don't know how to start explaining, so I just tell them everything—how I discovered Ingrid's journal under my bed, and only read a little at a time, and found a suicide note at the end. Susan and Mitch watch me intently as I explain all of this. At one point, Susan reaches over, and squeezes Mitch's hand.

"These are some pages," I say, placing the copies on the coffee table, "that I want you to have."

After the way they look at each other with tenderness, and at me with gratitude, and pick the copies up, I know that they don't expect anything more. They start with *Me on a Sunday Morning*, turn to *Dear Mom, I take it back*. Susan's chin trembles, Mitch takes her hand. Next, they read, *Dear Dad, I'm sorry*. And then they read the suicide note. I just sit quietly and let them go through them all. And even though the entries are obviously really meaningful to them, I still feel like they aren't enough. I mean, these are her *parents*, which means that they lost the most, more than I did, and I feel like they should have everything. I reach into my bag, ready to give it all up.

The bird on the cover is almost all chipped away now. And it feels surprisingly natural, even easy, when I place Ingrid's journal on the coffee table.

"You should have this, too," I say.

And then.

All at once I remember everything written inside—the way she wanted Jayson to hurt her, her anger at her mom, the creek, the guys. She didn't want them to know. I feel the blood draining from my face, get instantly nauseous. I'm not sure this is something I can take back.

Mitch studies my expression. He clears his throat. "We have so many of her diaries," he says. "You should see them. She kept them ever since she was a little girl. We even have a couple boxes in the garage full of them."

Susan touches the cover, but doesn't open it. "We've been reading some from her childhood, before she became ill. It's been a comfort to remember her that way—young and excited about her life." She shakes her head, picks up the journal, hands it back to me.

"If Ingrid wanted this to stay with you, then you should have it," she tells me, and she places it back in my hands. I slip it into its familiar compartment. Part of me is relieved, but later, as I walk out, my backpack feels heavier than it has ever felt before.

24

It is late and dark. Dylan is studying for finals, but I show up at her house and convince her to come out with me. I leave my parked car in front of her white picket fence and we walk to the theater. It is one of the first warm nights of the year. A million stars are out.

I'm relieved to find that the window hasn't been boarded up. I push the drape aside and we climb in.

"I can't see anything," Dylan says.

I unzip my backpack, pull out a flashlight.

When I click it on, Dylan says, "So this was part of the grand scheme of your day?"

I nod. Even with the flashlight, we have to feel our way down the aisle to the rows of seats. We choose two right in the center, and I tell Dylan everything about my day, from the moment I woke up until now.

"What about me?" she asks when I'm finished, and holds out her hands. I pull two folders out of my backpack, place one of them in her palms.

She doesn't open it. "Do you mind if I save it for later?"

I shake my head. "I gave you a lot," I say. "You can read them whenever you want to."

She slips the folder in her messenger bag. I open the second folder and pass it to Dylan. I shine the light for her as she flips through the photographs I borrowed from Ms. Delani.

"What I want," I say, "is to see these up there." I move the light away from the photographs and toward the white screen. "Do you think there's any way?"

Dylan squints.

"I mean, it might not be possible, but you're good at figuring this stuff out, right?"

I can almost see the procession of ideas filing, neatly and logically, behind her eyes. "Can you make them into slides?" she finally asks.

"Yes."

"We'll need a small battery-operated generator, but that's easy..."

She thinks a little longer. Then she says, "Sure. No problem."

She takes the flashlight from me, strides down the row of seats, and heads up the aisle. I hear her creak up the stairs to the projection room. Above me, through the projection window, the small beam of light appears—there she is, moving things around, untangling cords, making something out of nothing.

summer,
again

Like she did on the first day, Ms. Delani calls us according to where we sit, which means that I'll be last, but that's okay. She's taken down all the photographs from around the room, making space for our new ones. I choose a book to look in while I wait. Inside, all the pictures are of the photographer's mother.

By the time it's my turn, there are only a few minutes left of class. Ms. Delani comes out and thanks everyone for a good year, and tells them they can go, and says, "Caitlin, your turn."

I clutch my folder to my chest and follow her to the office.

She closes her grade book. We both know that next to my name are three Ds and a long line of zeros. But I have twelve new photographs in my hands.

She peers at me, apprehensively, through her glasses.

"Tell me you have something good to show me," she says.

I shift all my weight to one foot and stand there like an ostrich. "I have a series."

She exhales. "You have no idea how glad I am to hear that. Why don't you arrange them on the table. Call me out when you're finished."

So I go back into the classroom and lay them all on the big table under the window, where the light is perfect, and makes all the details show. Then I tell Ms. Delani I'm ready.

I don't look at her face as she evaluates my photographs. Instead, I look at my images with her.

I got slides made of Ingrid's photographs and used my savings to buy a small generator. Dylan rigged everything so that a single image covered the entire movie screen. It was incredible, how sharp and bright and vast they looked. Dylan sat above in the projection room while I worked downstairs with my tripod and camera. I had to expose each picture for a long time because, apart from the screen, the room was dark.

"These are . . ." Ms. Delani says, and doesn't finish.

"At first I didn't know if it would work," I say. "You know, photographing a photograph."

"But you've done so much more than that," Ms. Delani says. "Just by the act of enlarging the images, you've given her photographs heightened significance. They demand to be seen."

"Thanks," I say. "And the theater is important, too. It was her favorite place to go, but she never got to see the inside of it. I thought this would be a way of letting her in."

She nods. "Yes," she says. "When standing back and looking at them as a group, I see the lighted images first." She looks from photograph to photograph, saying, "The record player. The bedroom. The rain-spattered window. Bare feet. But then the details of the theater emerge and I see that there is much more going on here. The rows of empty seats are telling; they imply that though the images are enormous and commanding, they are going unseen. There is a secret here. Something private being exchanged between photographer and image."

"And there are the curtains, too," I say. "See this one?" I point to Ingrid's self-portrait with her camera. I pulled the heavy velvet curtains in a little on both sides so they cut the image off, narrowed the screen. "I was trying to make it seem like she was being hidden."

"Yes." Ms. Delani nods. "The light is still cast on the drapery, but the folds in the fabric obscure the image. As if the film is ending before it's finished."

"Like it might be able to tell me more if it weren't being forced away."

We study my photographs in silence for a little longer.

"Have you titled it?"

"Yes," I say. "It's called *Ghosts*."

"Caitlin," she says. "This is stunning work."

I feel so good it aches—not just because she's said it, but because I know it's true.

"Hold on." She disappears into her back office, and I remember the entry I brought for her in my backpack, the one where Ingrid talks about how much Ms. Delani inspired her. I had been planning on giving it to her today, but now I don't really want to. Maybe it's selfish, but I want this afternoon to be about me. So I grab the entry out of my bag and turn it facedown.

When Ms. Delani comes back into the room with a jar of push-pins in her hand, I say, "This is for you, but for later, so I'm just gonna drop it on your desk."

She nods, then she gathers my photographs and drags a chair to the front of the classroom. She hangs them there, one next to another, until they line the center wall.

The first pictures for the new year.

2

I'm perched on the edge of Henry's diving board, arms straight in the air.

"Dive!" Dylan shouts.

"Or stay," Taylor calls after her. "You look good up there. Look at your arms!"

"She *is* a carpenter," Dylan says.

"A what?"

"You didn't know that?"

I jump. The pool is so warm I barely feel the transition from air to water, but in a moment I'm immersed. I open my eyes to clear blue. Several pairs of board shorts and boys' legs, bikini bottoms, and red toenails. Turquoise tiled walls. I surface. Hear Henry ask, "So, your girlfriend. Is she hot?" Dylan answer, "She's gorgeous."

Finals have ended. This is the last-day-of-school party I always wanted to attend but never had the courage to. "Remember," Dylan said when we got to Henry's door an hour ago. "Drink beer, talk about who's hot, and spend some alone time with Taylor in the parents' bedroom."

"Are you serious?" I asked.

She shrugged. "Or, you know, you could just swim."

I swim. Slowly, deep enough to run my hands along the smooth white floor. Someone grazes my back. Taylor. We kiss underwater. When we surface, drops cling to the tips of his eyelashes.

"Hold still," I say. He closes his eyes and I lick them off. I taste chlorine, summer.

"You're a carpenter?"

"Yes."

"Dylan just told me. And a photographer?"

"Yes."

I think, *And a daughter, and a friend.* I shut my eyes and try to picture myself as all of these things. I can almost see it. I open my eyes to him, beaming.

"You're beautiful," he says.

"*You're* beautiful."

We swim together to the other side. I wish I had an underwater camera so I could capture the way his hair fans around his ears. The movement of his ankles as he kicks through the pool.

Hours pass. Taylor and Jayson are outside on the lawn chairs, having a silly conversation about superpowers. "You *already* run crazy fast," I hear Taylor say. "You should, like, shoot from here to the city in a millisecond."

"Zeptoseconds are faster," Dylan informs me. We're across the backyard, sprawled out on the grass.

"What's it like when you make out with Maddy?" I ask.

Dylan's eyebrows raise. "That's an unexpected question."

"It shouldn't be," I say. "We've talked about everything else. Why not this?"

She shrugs.

"This is what most friends talk about," I say. "Let's just try it."

She turns onto her back and looks up. The sun is setting. Streaks of orange and pink line the hills.

"Let's start with Maddy. Give me two adjectives to describe how Maddy kisses."

Dylan covers her face with her hands and grins. I edge closer to her.

"Confident," she says. "Graceful." She peeks at me between fingers.

"You're blushing!" I yelp. "You've never blushed before in your entire life."

"That's not true." She laughs.

"Why is she blushing?" Taylor yells from across the yard.

"And Taylor?" she whispers.

"Miraculous," I whisper back. "Sweet."

———

More hours pass. People leave. The house quiets. Taylor and Jayson and Henry and Dylan and I are outside, sharing a pizza Henry
had delivered. Everyone is talking, laughing, but Henry just eats
and stares off into the night. We finish the pizza. The night air be-
comes cooler. I walk inside the house. Henry is in the foyer, sitting
on the edge of the fountain under the family portrait. He had been
so quiet that I didn't even notice when he slipped away. I pull my
balled-up, yellow sweater from the depths of my backpack. Instead
of going back outside right away, I sit down on the fountain next
to him.

We don't say anything. He stares at his hands; I tug on the ends
of my sweater drawstrings. Then he dips his hand in the fountain
and splashes water on his family portrait.

"Life is shit," he tells me.

I nod. "Maybe."

His face is red with anger or embarrassment, I can't tell which. I
glance at the portrait, then back to his face when I feel him watching me.

"But not all the time," I say. "I don't think all the time."

3

My treehouse is finished. Actually, *finished* might not be the right
word. I'll say this instead: my treehouse is complete.

It has a wide, sturdy ladder that rises ten feet from the ground. It
has six walls, and an opening for a door, and big openings on each
side to let in light and air. The tree trunk rises through the middle
of the wide floor, its bark thick and rough and strong. The ceiling
is seven feet high—I had to stand on a stepladder to build it, and
my dad helped me with the hard-to-reach places, by holding beams
steady as I hammered, by helping me lift what was too heavy.

Mom had the Persian rug cleaned for me, and now the colors

are even more vibrant than they were when I found it. On a small branch just outside a window, I've hung the wood-and-glass hummingbird feeder. I bought a really comfortable, cushy chair from a sidewalk sale, and placed it in a corner. I used the wine crates from the garage as little tables, put a vase with flowers on one, next to a picture frame with Ingrid's self-portrait in it, and a couple candles in my dad's old, hippyish candleholders. I bought sixteen simple black frames from a store in the strip mall, to frame my *Ghosts* series. Then I hung them, three on five of the walls, the last one above the door. When I invited them up to see, Dad actually cried, and Mom gazed at them with this proud look, like I just painted the *Mona Lisa.*

Tomorrow is demolition, and it's also the *treehouse-warming party,* as my parents insist on calling it. Maddy's coming out from the city, and Dylan's bringing some of her mom's amazing food, and Taylor and Jayson, and, of course, my parents, who have been going on and on about the dessert they're making with rhubarb from their garden. I left a message for Ms. Delani, asking her to come. She left me a message back saying she would love to.

I've already picked out the music, and set up the plates and silverware, so I have nothing to do but wait. I turn the music on with the volume low, stretch out on the rug, and fade in and out of sleep for a while. Each time I wake up, I look through the skylight to see how the clouds have shifted.

4

I wake up at 2 A.M., only five hours before the demolition starts, and know I have to go to the theater one more time. I leave a note for my parents on my bed, slip on some jeans and a hoodie and my green Converses, grab my bag, and creep out the door.

It's pitch-black when I get there, and I silently thank my dad for forcing me to keep a flashlight in my trunk. I park in front of the library, use the flashlight to find my way to the broken window, throw my bag through it, and crawl in after.

I pull Ingrid's journal from my bag, and rip out the first page, careful to tear it cleanly. I put the drawing *Me on a Sunday Morning* in a folder in my bag. Then I head up to the projection room for the box of marquee letters. I want to send her a message.

If I hadn't spent all year dangling from tree branches, I would be terrified right now. I'm climbing to the top of the rickety ladder that has surely been leaning against the wall in the break room for years, with a flashlight under one arm, the bag of letters under the other. Thankfully, there is a ledge beneath the marquee where I can set everything down. It is a still, warm night. I have no idea how I'll be able to fit everything I have to say to her in this small space. I take down the old words, GO DBYE & THA K YOU, and think of what to write.

I think of everything: red earrings that looked like buttons. Stealing glances of her journal from over her shoulder, glimpsing words and phrases and parts of drawings. Grooves in her fingers from squeezing her pen too tight. The way I felt when she looked at me from behind the lens: awkward, pretty, necessary. Ditching school to do nothing. Blue veins and pale skin. *You are such a nerd.* Red light of the darkroom across her concentrated face. A quiet hill, damp grass under our bare feet. Scar tissue spelling *ugly.* Clear blue eyes. *I'll go wherever you go.* Tall glasses of champagne. *Hold still. We look amazing.* Dancing in a yellow dress. The creek. *You might be looking for reasons but there are no reasons.* Slipping nail polish into pockets. *I don't want to hurt you or anybody so please just forget about me.*

I sort through the letters and pull out what I need for the beginning. They snap easily into place. And even though I thought I would need every letter, I finish the first sentence and realize that it's all I have left to say.

I MISS YOU.

Carefully, I feel my way down. I return the bag to the projection room, where my backpack waits for me. I take out the journal again. The Wite-Out bird is completely chipped off now. I set the journal on a shelf between a few books and some old film reels. I stand up, walk to the doorway, and shine my light on the black cover for the last time. From here, it looks like any other book.

5

I wake up in my jeans and sweater. When I think about last night, it seems foggy and distant.

I look in my backpack, just to be sure. The zipper pocket is empty.

My parents have a cereal bowl set out at my spot at the table when I come down for breakfast. They are sitting together, reading different sections of the paper.

"We packed you a lunch," Dad says. Mom hands me a brown paper bag. I peer inside. Peanut butter and jelly, an apple, a granola bar.

"Aw," I say. "Like sixth grade."

Mom rolls her eyes. Dad rumples my hair.

I only have a couple minutes to get out the door. I eat my cereal, brush my teeth, say good-bye to my parents, and start walking, for the last time, to the theater.

At the corner across the street from the strip mall, I hear a low rumble come from the road. A long row of semitrucks are coming toward me. I watch them move slowly down the main road, one by one, like a funeral procession. A driver in a red hat waves. I lift my hand.

It's only a little past seven, but the sun already feels hot. Far ahead of me, the trucks slow and turn right, toward the theater. I follow.

By the time I get there, a crowd already stretches around the block, and the semitrucks are unloaded. Towering over everything is a huge orange machine. It looks a like metal dinosaur. For a minute, it makes me forget about skyscrapers and mountains—I'm sure it's bigger than anything on Earth.

I ease my way through the crowds of old people and guys with lawn chairs and moms holding little kids, until I'm right up along the caution tape. It's so strange to have all these people here, in this place that I always thought of as a secret. I wonder how many of them ever came here before today, and what this demolition means to them.

I sit cross-legged in the street with people all around me.

Then the orange machine comes to life.

It rumbles to a start, inches massively forward. Its mechanical neck raises to the sky, reaches at least thirty feet above me, before it crashes down on the side of the theater.

It all happens so fast after that. Powerful metal jaws at the end of the neck eat through the wall in only minutes, and then the machine rolls into the theater and attacks it from the inside, sending the back wall crashing in. The ground beneath me shakes. A man sprays water from a fire hose, stopping the dust from blowing into our faces. The air smells strong and toxic, but as I reach to cover my face, I remember this thing about Ingrid that I haven't thought of for so long.

Once, my mom was taking us somewhere and we had to fill the car up with gas, and Ingrid rolled her window down as we pulled into the station. She stuck her head out, breathed in deep.

What are you doing? I asked.

I love the smell of gasoline, she said, exhaling.

I made a face. All I knew about gas was what my parents grumbled about—it was too expensive, Mom hated getting it on her hands.

Ingrid leaned out the window. *Try it,* she said. *You'll love it.*

I didn't. *You have problems,* I told her, and she laughed and inhaled again.

I recognize the gasoline scent now, mixed with the familiar must. And as the machines chomp away at the theater, and walls collapse deafeningly, I breathe in the smell of change. It isn't as bad as I thought it would be, or maybe it's so bad it's intoxicating—I'm not sure which. Behind me, a baby wails, but I can hardly hear her over the noise.

Before I've prepared myself, the machine approaches the front of the theater. It stops right next to the marquee, raises its neck, opens its jaws, and my heart grows too big for my chest. My vision blurs. It crashes down. The roof crumbles. I imagine Ingrid's journal tumbling from its shelf, pages flapping in the air like wings, hitting the ground face open. Water from the fire hose drenches the paper until the colors blend together, the drawings lose their shape, the words turn indecipherable.

A hand squeezes my shoulder. I look up. It's Jayson.

He lowers himself next to me and pulls a pack of tissues from his pocket.

I don't think I can speak yet. I try to force myself to smile, and it's easier than I thought it would be. It lets out some of the pressure. He smiles back. The last wall collapses and I'm still smiling, blotting tears from my face with Jayson's tissues, watching the wood splinter under the massive machine, the theater becoming less and less what it used to be.

After it's over and the ground has stopped shaking, a dozen men flood into the site, filling the trucks with what's left. The crowd starts to pack up and leave.

"Were you here for the whole thing?" Jayson asks.

I nod. "Were you?"

"Most of it."

Soon, the crowd is gone except for Jayson and me.

"I'm gonna go run now," he says, standing.

I look at the empty block. It's already hard to believe that a theater once stood there.

"I'm staying a while longer."

Jayson says, "See you at your place," and jogs off. I watch the men as they work. They shovel wood into one truck, copper pipes into another. They break up the concrete from the foundations, wheel it away. I unpack my lunch and eat while they work. It's been hours since my breakfast, but I haven't felt hungry until now. Slowly, the blocks get emptier, the workers drive away. It's about four in the afternoon when a man comes by to take the caution tape down.

"Show's over," he says to me, smiling. "Afraid there's no more excitement for the day."

He bunches the tape in his hands. His eyes are friendly.

"Was it your first demolition?" he asks.

"Yeah," I say.

"So . . ." He sweeps his arm across the open blocks. "What did you think?"

I don't really know what I think, so I open my mouth to tell him that. But what I end up saying is, "It was amazing."

And I mean it.

"Sure was, wasn't it? I've been doing this for more than twenty years, and it still gives me a thrill."

He looks down at me and scratches his head. I know exactly what I look like to him—a crazy teenager just lingering here for no reason.

I pull my legs to my chest and squint up at him. I lift a hand to block the sun.

"I'm just remembering things," I offer.

And that seems to clear something up. He nods and turns toward the empty space, as though he'll see what I'm thinking about, projected in the air.

6

The night before Ingrid died, we studied for our biology finals halfheartedly on the floor of my room. We kept getting distracted, saying *I love this song* whenever something good came on the radio, turning it up and forgetting about our textbooks open to unread pages in front of us.

Ingrid said, "Fuck bio. Let's plan our futures," and her voice had all this urgency, this forced lightness, that I only partly noticed.

I shut my book and said, "Okay. You start."

"*You* start."

I turned onto my back and looked up at the ceiling. I said, "I want to go away somewhere for college."

"Like the East Coast?"

"Like Oregon or Montana."

"Do you want snow or ocean?"

"There's a glacier in Montana. I heard that all the glaciers in America are melting. They'll be gone before we're old."

"So snow?"

"I don't know," I said. "I heard the Oregon coast is amazing."

"So ocean?"

"I don't know. I guess I can't decide."

"What will you major in?"

I said, "I have no idea."

She said, "You like English, right?"

"Yeah," I said, "but I just like to read for fun."

She said, "Well, you like art."

I said, "Yes. I like art."

"So art, then."

"Okay."

"Maybe you'll have a gallery show."

"Or just go to a lot of galleries."

"You'll be brilliant," Ingrid said. "Maybe you'll be a professor or something, and all your students will have crushes on you."

I smiled. I turned over to face her.

I said, "What about you?"

She shrugged. "You know. I'll photograph, travel."

"But what about college?"

I looked at her as I waited for her to answer. If there was any doubt in her face, I didn't see it.

Finally, she said, "I'll go wherever you go."

I smacked the bio book in her lap. "If we even get *into* college."

When she laughed, I laughed, too, and I hardly listened to her, never thought: *This is the last time I'll hear her laughing.*

"We'll get in," she said. "It's gonna be great. You're gonna be great."

And at some point, when she got up to leave, I must have looked away, and she must have slid her journal under my bed, and I must have thought some random thought, not knowing what was coming.

7

I sit at the demolition site for a long time. The caution-tape man leaves, and so do all the other men, carrying away pieces of the giant machine, remnants of the theater, until all that's left is daylight and dust, and a level, empty street.

It isn't the happy ending that Ingrid and I had dreamed up, but it's all a part of what I'm working through. The way life changes. The way people and things disappear. Then appear, unexpectedly, and hold you close.

I stand up and unzip my backpack. I pull out the tripod and arrange my shot: a newly barren street. In the distance, the undeveloped hills of Los Cerros. Dust from what used to be shimmers as it settles to the ground. I adjust my focus until it is on a spot several feet from where I'm standing.

I set the timer, and step out in front of the camera.

I face the lens, walk backward until I reach the spot I focused on—close enough that I will fill most of the frame, far enough that my whole body will be in the photograph. The timer ticks faster and faster, getting ready to take the picture, and I stand straight, breathe deep, and exhale as the ticking stops. I hold completely still. I can almost feel it—the shutter opens, the film gains density, absorbs light, and there I am.

This is what I look like: an almost seventeen-year-old, caught standing, arms at my sides, feet flat on gravel, in the middle of an empty street. Straight auburn hair that hasn't been cut for a year, now splitting at the ends where it grazes my back. A dozen small freckles on the bridge of my nose, left over from childhood. Sharp elbows and knees, strong arms from pounding and lifting. White bra straps showing through a white tank top, dirty jeans from spending a day in the dust. Small mouth, without lip gloss, without a smile. Brown eyes open wide and unguarded, alert in spite of a series of sleepless nights. An expression that's hard to pin down—part longing, part sorrow, part hope.

acknowledgments

I am deeply fortunate to know too many wonderful people to mention by name on these pages. To all of you: my deepest gratitude for making my life so full of warmth and love.

To my mother, Deborah Hovey-LaCour, and my father, Jacques La-Cour (who is neither a pirate nor a mathematician): my list of thank you's could go on forever. I'll be brief, and say this: thank you for always believing in me. To my little brother, Jules LaCour: thank you for being such an excellent person, and for making me laugh so hard and so often. To my grandparents, Joseph and Elizabeth LaCour: thank you for your unwavering love, and for teaching me the theory of relativity.

To Sherry and Hal Stroble: thank you for your love and generosity. I am so lucky, for so many reasons, to be your daughter-in-law.

To my editor, Julie Strauss-Gabel: thank you for bringing out the best in this novel, and, in the process, teaching me so much about writing. To everyone at Dutton: thank you for caring so much about this book. To my lovely agent, Sara Crowe: you make it so easy.

To Jessica Jacobs, one of this book's very first readers: thank you for being so confident that my scattered, fragmented scenes would someday become a novel, and for your sound advice and encouragement through every stage of this process. To Vanessa Micale, Rachel Murawski, Evan Pricco, and Eli Harris: thank you for your insights, your support, and your friendship. To Eric Levy: I don't know how I would have written a query letter without you. To Charlotte Ribar and Sophie Smyer: reading your comments delighted and helped me more than you could imagine. To Mandy Harris: thank you for getting my manuscript ready to send out into the world. To Mia Nolting: thank you for pouring so much artistic energy into this book, even before you were hired to do it. To my best friend, Amanda Krampf: thank you for being my high school partner in crime. I'm so glad we met at that bus stop.

To my teachers from elementary school through graduate school: you worked so hard, and you were wonderful. I am especially thankful to George Hegarty, Dr. Ruth Saxton, and Yiyun Li. To Kathryn Reiss: thank you for teaching me about children's literature, and for your valuable feedback and encouragement on this book. And to Isabel: thank you for my first fan letter.

Finally, to Kristyn Stroble: thank you for reading every word of every draft, and for crying at all the right parts. Most of all, thank you for making me so happy. Without you, this would not have been possible.

Questions for Discussion

- In the immediate aftermath of Ingrid's suicide, how does Caitlin deal with her grief? In what ways do her methods of dealing with grief change as the year progresses? Are her coping mechanisms healthy?

- Describe the relationship between Caitlin and her parents. How do they help Caitlin in healing? Could they have been more helpful?

- Why do you think Ingrid left behind her journal for Caitlin?

- How does Ingrid's journal change Caitlin's perspective on Ingrid? On their friendship?

- How did you feel about the character of Ms. Delani? Do you feel she handled her own grief appropriately?

- Discuss the role of photography in the book. What do the characters' ideas about beauty and art show about themselves?

- How do Ingrid's journal pages and sketches enhance the story? Do you keep a journal or sketchbook? Why?

- Discuss the new relationships Caitlin forms throughout this book. Do these friendships form because of or in spite of what happened with Ingrid?

- What is the significance of the tree house for Caitlin? How does it help her cope with loss?

- What were some of the signs that Ingrid was depressed? Was there anything Caitlin could have done to help Ingrid?

- Why do you think the title of the book is *Hold Still*? What does it mean for Caitlin?

Author Q & A

You are a high school English teacher. Did your students influence your novel?

Actually, I started writing *Hold Still* in graduate school, before I ever seriously considered teaching high school. I was working on a novel for adults, but as soon as I began writing this one, it just took off. I was twenty-two, which felt like a perfect age at which to write about high school—I was distant enough to have a clear perspective of what it was like but close enough to still remember vividly all the excitements and longings and disappointments of that time.

When you started writing Hold Still, *did you have a clear idea of what your novel would be about?*

I knew that it would be about grief. When I was in ninth grade, one of my classmates took his life. I didn't know him well, but learning of his death remains one of the most profoundly sad and confusing events of my childhood. I remember sitting with a group of other kids trying to make sense out of what had happened. It is still a mystery to me. So even though this story is not autobiographical, I felt compelled to write about something that I wrestled with in my own teenage years—the journey to finding oneself again in the wake of a great loss.

What were your other inspirations?

Art, specifically photography, is a major part of *Hold Still*. Right before I wrote the first pages, I visited my mom's classroom to look at her students' work. (My mom is a high school photography teacher.) One image still haunts me. It is a black-and-white, dramatically lit photograph of a girl with the words *ugly, fat, stupid* carved into her stomach. The photograph is heartbreaking, but it is also beautiful. I was simultaneously troubled by the image and in awe of the photographer's work. This photograph influenced my writing in so many ways. The girl in the image inspired the character of Ingrid, and the act of photographing became one of Caitlin's passions. Throughout the book, even as Caitlin is struggling, she is finding joy in creating art.

Did you do research when writing this book?

Initially, I did quite a bit of research on depression and suicide. And though I'm sure that some of what I learned found its way into the book, I realized later that it was more important that I understand Ingrid as a character than know how to diagnose her. What both Ingrid and Caitlin love is photography, so I took a class through U. C. Berkeley and learned to develop black-and-white film and make prints in a darkroom. It's thrilling.

So now that you are around high school students all day, do you think they will influence your next book?

Maybe. But don't tell them. They might ask for extra credit.

Behind the Music

I often hear from readers who ask me what Davey put on Caitlin's mix tape. I love this question, not only because it's exciting to know that people want to inhabit Caitlin's world a little more, but also because mix tapes are some of my favorite things. This will make me sound like a Luddite but I'll say it anyway: playlists are cool, but mix tapes were better. They took forever to make because you had to plan the order carefully and listen to each full song as it was being recorded. I remember staying up late on school nights fast-forwarding and rewinding and lying on my carpet as the songs played. I resisted burning CDs until my freshman year in college when my best friend confessed that the tape I had spent a whole day making her was still in its box, unheard, because not even her car had a tape player anymore. I was crushed, and then I went out and bought blank CDs.

Fortunately, Caitlin's car (which happens to be identical to my first car, furry seat covers and all) does have a tape player, and Caitlin, unlike any sixteen-year-old I know, has the pleasure of having a mix tape. I like to think of Caitlin sitting up all night in her car listening to these songs and their lyrics; they are full of heartbreak and loss and friendship and love and hope. I hope you enjoy them.

"Close to Me" by The Cure
"Les Étoiles Secrètes" by Ida
"I'm Not Going Anywhere Tonight" by Owen
"We Will Become Silhouettes" by The Postal Service
"More Adventurous" by Rilo Kiley
"Get Me Away from Here, I'm Dying" by Belle and Sebastian
"Bowl of Oranges" by Bright Eyes
"A Fond Farewell" by Elliott Smith
"Call It Off" by Tegan and Sara
"I Feel It All" by Feist

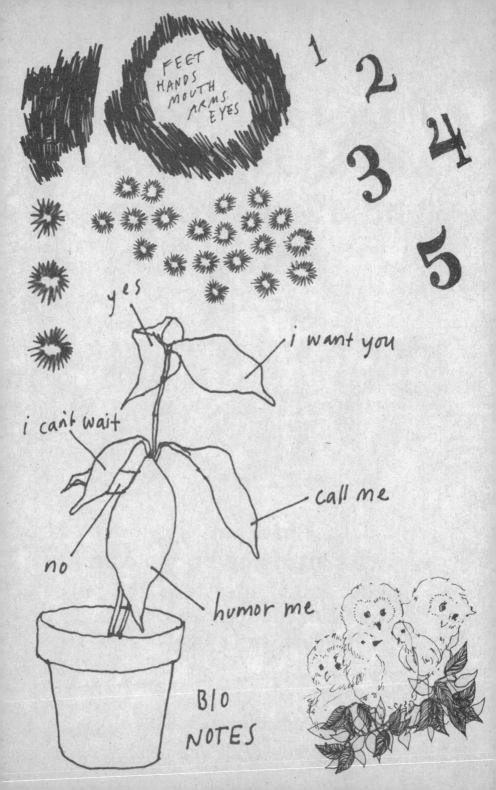

YOU DON'T EVEN
HAVE TO SAY IT
CAUSE IT'S OBVIOUS
EITHER WAY

HOLD HOLD
Hold
HOLD

7
6
8 9 0

100,000 SECRET
HEARTS WAITING

COMING
OUT
WHOLE

SECRET

DRAWN ON THE BUS